DINOSAURS & SNOW ANGELS

Early Stories

Mary Taylor

Copyright © 2021 Mary Taylor

All rights reserved

This book is a work of fiction. Any references to real people, real products, real places or historical events are used fictitiously. Other names, characters, places and events are the products of the author's imagination, and any resemblance to actual events, places or persons living or dead is entirely coincidental.

No part of this book may be reproduced, or stored in a retrieval system, or transmitted in any form or by any means, electronic, mechanical, photocopying, recording, or otherwise, without express written permission of the author.

ISBN: 979-8-7290-1634-1
www.blackstonefinn.com

For my beloved

*"O blessed vision! Happy child!
Thou art so exquisitely wild,
I think of thee with many fears
For what may be thy lot in future years."*

WILLIAM WORDSWORTH, TO H.C. SIX YEARS
OLD (1807)

CONTENTS

Title Page
Copyright
Dedication
Epigraph

The 1970s	1
DINOSAURS & SNOW ANGELS	3
WE ARE	29
SPAGHETTI & BULLIES	43
MIDOL & TIGER BEAT	77
FOUND & LOST	87
DEATH AT 14	119
...	147
Emotional Imprints Series	149
Acknowledgements	151

THE 1970S

Book 1

DINOSAURS & SNOW ANGELS

Three days past Christmas, the snow begins to fall again. I search for my mother in our cavernous, cold house. My oldest brother William Jr., his wife Hope, and their son Little Will left that morning. Dad was back at work. Mom was somewhere, and I was cold and searching for her.

The twelve-foot tree still in the sunroom, but now, no colorful presents beneath it, just dry needles and fallen tinsel.

My nephew Little Will was only three years

younger and more of a brother to me than my real brothers ever were.

During the holidays, we transformed this cavernous cold house into our magical playground:

In the wine cellar we were spies searching for top secret information hidden in dusty secret places.

In the living room, the space underneath the long couch was our escape tunnel from East to West Berlin. We were spies with rug burn on our knees.

In the ballroom, we were Batman and Robin and Dad's WWII field phone became our Batphone.

The original owners custom-built the house in the 1920s with a third floor for their cooks and maids. A private stairway from the third floor was the perfect hiding place to spy on whatever was happening in the kitchen.

Different from the rest of the house, the walls were the color of pistachio ice cream, the wooden steps were painted that same color with shiny, black rubber strips nailed over them instead of carpet.

I search for her in the kitchen.

"Mom?"
She is not there either.

* * *

Just a few nights before that same kitchen was full of warm bread smells and laughter.

Hiding in that pistachio-green stairway, Little Will and I played "Dinosaur" a game where everyone in the family was a Dinosaur by number.

"Dinosaur 1 is at the kitchen table," I said.

"Where's Dinosaur 2? Let me looooook!"

"Shhh," I say, "they'll hear us."

Dinosaur 2 is William Jr., Little Will's dad, my oldest brother. He was not there.

We strain to hear the table of women. All the women of the family are in the kitchen except for me.

I was not yet a woman, but rather just a girl, a skinny colt-legged tomboy with long hair and my father's square fingers. I couldn't wait to be all grown-up like my sister Lydia and my sister-in-law Hope.

My nineteen-year-old sister Lydia home from college for winter break shares that she has decided that she wants to major in Russian studies. She had always been excellent at languages and lived in France for a year in upper school.

"Lydia, your father is paying for you to get an education for your future, how will Russian be of any use?"

"I was thinking maybe D.C., you know, maybe intelligence," Lydia says.

"I was stationed in Washington, D.C. during the war and I could have gone to MIT after, but I went to work instead."

Lydia rolled her eyes, "I know mom, you have told that story a thousand times."

"Well, Hope and Kate may not have heard it. I had been offered a full scholarship, and was the only woman they admitted for a masters in engineering. I would have gone on to be a civil engineer, but I chose to get a job instead, and that's where I met your father."

Mother wearing her big, puffy, stove mittens, pulls out fresh loaves of bread from the oven. Powdered loaves raised high and golden they spill over their pans.

She sets them lovingly on the cooling racks next to the stove. Like many women of her generation, she was expected to marry and raise a family.

"How did you and Mr. Lawrence meet?" Hope asked.

Mom giggled like the young woman she once was and said,

"We met at a summer company picnic. Mind you, I was still pretty new to the job, and walking by this group of loud, arrogant men who were drinking beers - "

"Oh no, here we go," Lydia said.

"Lydia, hush. Well, I heard this one man say the darndest thing, he said, 'Fellas, there's *nothing worse* than a Pembroker or a W.A.C.'"

She took off her oven mitts, and placed linen napkins in front of each of the three women.

"Well, I stopped. Turned to him and said, 'Sir, I don't know who you are, but I will have you know I graduated from Pembroke *and* I proudly served in the Women's Army Corps!'"

Hope laughed, "Then what happened?"

"I got more potato salad," she laughed, "He took me on a lovely date, we were crazy for each other, of course. Within three months he asked my father's permission for my hand in marriage. He proposed and we were married within a year."

"And then William Junior appeared on the scene soon after," Lydia chuckled.

"Lydia," mom scolded, "why do you imply such things? I was a virgin until my wedding night, and your father is the only man I have ever loved."

"That's romantic," Kate said almost too quiet for us eavesdropping spies to hear.

"Yes, quite," mom said, "and he was so handsome with that jet-black hair and those blue eyes."

"Things are changing now mom, women want careers outside the home," Lydia said.

"My mother, your grandmother, did not even have the right to vote. She sold encyclopedias door-to-door to pay for her college education."

"She told me that she was forced to quit her job when she got married," Lydia said.

"Forced to?" Kate asked.

"Yes," Lydia continued, "Grandma taught Spanish after she graduated from college, and back then it was against the law for married women to teach. Wasn't that it mom?"

"Yes," mom said as she smoothed her

apron. "You girls are very lucky to have many more opportunities than your grandmothers ever had."

Years later in the rubble of the big-truth, mother would confide in me just how much the "what ifs" had haunted her. *Wasted potential, it's the curse of being born at the wrong time.*

The women looked at each other in silence for a long time. So quiet, I could hear Little Will breathing. I was sure we'd get caught spying.

"So I guess I'm the only woman of the family who never went to college," Hope said in a loud voice.

Hope, my sister-in-law, has her back to us secret spies hiding in the stairway. The kitchen chair dwarfs under her large curvaceous body.

Lydia speaks some Russian words in a low tone of voice. She animates a joke that I cannot understand but Hope does.

Hope's high-pitched laugh is full and round like the rich sound of the brass handbells played every year at my school's Christmas Vespers.

She laughs with her whole body. Head

back, her shoulders shake up and down. She tilts back in her chair as if she needs more room for all that joy inside her.

My mother with her proper lipstick smile is the conductor of the kitchen, the perfect hostess. She listens to these women, smiling with the occasional girlish giggle. A measured laugh just big enough, but never "unladylike".

And then there is Kate, tall, quiet, her thin body reed-like, she sits angled in her chair, across the table from Lydia. Her legs crossed with a flat palm hidden between her thighs. Kate is the wife of my other brother George who was fourteen when I was born. Brilliant George had a mean-streak wider than his perfect Ivy League lettered life would ever let on. Like him, Kate will be forever holding everything inside.

It is Hope's laughter, Hope's lifeforce that fills the kitchen that night with warmth and joy. Over thick slices of warm bread and butter, my sister, Mom and Kate can't help but laugh and smile for Hope's happiness is contagious.

Little Will and I hiding on the back stairs now convinced we are unseen and unheard as we witness these women through the small crack in the door ajar.

"Let me see," Little Will whispers "what are they laughing about?"

His small hand reaches for the glass doorknob. I move over to sit down on the stairs. His brown corduroys bunched and baggy, his belt over a missed belt loop, and his socks half-off from our earlier escape from East Berlin through the secret tunnel under the couch.

After Little Will was put to bed, me in my sock feet padded quietly back towards the kitchen. Not from the back stairs, but slow, through the main hallway. They were drinking tea now, my sister holding a thick handmade blue mug she made in her ceramics class.

I walked in on some adult talk: something about Hope's father, whom they called "Pop", not allowing any "bastards" to come into his family. Something about Little Will being a mistake. When they saw me the room got quiet real fast.

I sat up on my sister's lap and reached for a slice of the fresh bread. I spread the butter on thick and slow, the question burning in my mind slipped out.

"What's a bastard?"

My sister cleared her throat behind me choking down a laugh.

"Nothing," Mom said. "It's nothing."

"It's a child born out of wedlock," Hope said.

"*Conceived* out of wedlock," Lydia said.

"Was Little Will a bastard?"

"No, honey, he wasn't," Hope said.

My mother's back to me, she's doing something at the stove. Kate sips her tea without making a sound.

Smells of bread, the butter soft on my knife, the room got heavy with quiet.

I took a bite wondering if I should ask the question. I was always asking questions, and much of the time got in a lot of trouble for it.

My face got hot as I chewed the delicious bread, swallowed, then asked,

"Was he a mistake?"

"No," Hope said, "he wasn't."

My sister patted her hands hard on my hips and bounced me up and down on her knees.

"But *you* were," she said in a sing-songy voice.

My mother jumped. "*Lydia*, that's enough."

Then turning to me her face hard, "Young lady, you ask too many questions!"

I looked over at Hope. Her eyes reaching for mine. Her lips curved in a sad closed half-smile. I recognized Hope then as the only truth in the room.

"Is the baklava cool enough now?" Kate asked.

My mother welcomed the diversion, and put a pan of sticky flakey pastry on the table,

"Yes Kate, would you please cut that for us?"

Mom handed Kate a fancy knife specifically for cutting pastry without damaging the pan.

I watched Kate's steady, quiet hand cut diagonal lines into small sweet triangles.

Mistake?

Bastard?

Something about Pop not wanting her to have it. No Little Will? There was a possibility that he might not have been? I could not imagine life without him. He was the brother to me that mine never were.

I jumped off my sister's lap, and went into the living room, to do something I did not like to do: Math.

I knew it took nine months to make a baby. I knew when he was born, and I knew when Hope and my brother got married. With a pencil and paper I got my answer: they made him before they got married.

Seeing those numbers penciled-out on paper the mysterious concept of sex became real to me in a way it hadn't before. I realized what my brother and Hope did together made Little Will, and they made him before they got married.

My body tingled with the delicious thrill that I discovered a secret. Something that had been too taboo to discuss in front of me. Something mom did not want me to know.

We had some sex education at school in the form of "It's what mommy and daddy do when they love each other" and Judy Blume's *Are You There God, It's Me Margaret*. And then there were the ink anatomy diagrams that made sex look as gross as the black lung images they showed to warn us about the dangers of smoking.

Being an all girls progressive school, our teacher did her best to be candid and forthcoming, but sometimes even she would blush at our questions and comments. Like when Janey announced that boys and girls are not really that different at all because she tried to pee standing up like her brother does and it "kinda works."

Ms. Gillhern said that was fine to do at home, but admonished her to not try that in the school bathrooms. This only resulted in further nervous whispers and giggles.

This new information about Little Will was different. It had the heavy feelings of responsibility and seriousness, curiosity and fear all bundled together. More powerful than what I had heard at school or even saw in the books my sister brought back from France. In the 1970s there was no talk of "safe sex" yet, and birth control was not openly discussed either. Sex was still such a mystery.

Having much older siblings had created a longing to discover the secrets and mysteries of growing-up from an early age, but now I had a new feeling: a profound sense of fear.

Fear.

And doubt.

That night when Hope tucked me in under my winter flannel sheets and down comforter, she placed her hand on my head and ran her fingers slow across my scalp and through my long hair. My whole body immediately relaxed at her touch.

"Was Little Will a mistake?" I asked.

"No," Hope said gently, "I told you he wasn't."

"But you weren't married...when you made him?"

"That's right," Hope said, "your brother and I were so much in love we couldn't wait."

Her voice was soft and kind. I knew in that moment I could ask her anything.

"But Pop told you not to have him?"

"Yes," she said, "he forbid me to have a child at my age. I had just turned seventeen, and that was too young, I was supposed to go on to college, so my parents arranged for me to go to Paris to...to..."

The light from the hallway on Hope's face, her eyes got shiny.

"...but then your brother and I went to talk to your father. We were both terrified. He sat us down and asked us if we loved each other. We said yes, and he was kind and supportive. He gave us his blessing and told us that if we wanted to get married he would help us any way he could. Your father was wonderful to us. He still is."

"I'm glad you got married," I said, "I can't imagine life without you or Little Will."

With her hand still on my head, she turned away and bent her cheek towards her shoulder, wiping her tears.

Then, smiling big, her teeth perfectly straight and beautiful she said,

"Listen, have you ever made snow angels?"

"I don't think so," I said.

"That's what we are going to do tomorrow. You and Little Will and I are going to make snow angels out on the boulevard."

Her hand bigger and warmer than my mom's. Soft and yielding yet firm. I started to drift-off to dreams of Christopher Robin and Pooh making snow angels in the Hundred Acre Wood.

❋ ❋ ❋

And now Hope's gone.

They're all gone.

The living room is so much bigger now, empty with memories. The same living room where just the day before Little Will and I played catch with a gold damask pillow from the couch. *I'm gonna be like Joe Namath, and play football!*

Remembering Little Will's challenge, *betcha can't walk on your hands*, I launch into a handstand, walk six feet on my hands and then cartwheel though the grey light of afternoon snowfall and soft shadows.

Giggles and Legos, and headstands on pillows. Every day for that whole week Little Will and I created magical worlds in which we would play and laugh until that time mom declared,

"Nap time! You two are overtired. Time to go lie down!"

"But mom it's not even lunchtime!"

"You two are too excited and are being too silly, you must be overtired. I will call you both when lunch is ready."

And we were sent off to our rooms as if being punished with a "time out" which was a new parenting technique in the '70s.

Instead of "the strap" which was used on generations before, a child would be sent to their room to think about what they had done and then respond accordingly. We were not being punished for anything wrong officially and yet we were. I sat on my pink bedspread with my constant companions of Leo, Teddy, Rupert and Peter Rabbit and the shame seeped in.

It was as if our happiness made her unhappy. And too much happiness expressed upset mom.

This would be one of the marks, a part of that larger imprint that said *there were negative consequences for too much happiness.*

I told Peter Rabbit, "I'd better tone it down a bit. I need to set a good example for Little Will, he's just a baby."

Sitting in my pink and white bedroom on my bed I shared with stuffed animals, I thought about Hope. She never scolded us for being silly or happy or laughing too much.

* * *

I wanted to go back in time. Such a strange thing is time. Seemingly shorter and faster when Hope and Little Will were around. Always longer before and after their visits.

The house swallows me. I walk slow up the long, wide carpeted staircase. Tall cathedral-like stained-glass windows tower over the landing. Gray winter light throws soft colors on the oak wainscoting and gold Berber carpet.

My small hand slides up the banister that just yesterday, Little Will and I were sliding down. Our game was to go as fast as you could and stop yourself just before your tailbone would hit that large wooden acorn at the bottom using our hands as breaks. The banister cools under my cold hand as I walk up the stairs.

"Mom, where are you?"

I turn at the landing and take the last four stairs. The door to my parent's master bedroom is closed.

I knock and hear a distant 'come in'.

The large quiet fills the largest bedroom of the house. My parent's master bedroom runs the length of the house complete with huge bath and separate his and her wardrobe rooms for dressing.

Mother stands over by the bay window in her burgundy wool suit, complete with stockings and dressy heels. She always looks nice. I walk up next to her. Her lipstick the same burgundy red to match her wool suit.

She is cleaning up the Christmas wrapping. The large metal radiator between her and the bay window, I put my hands on the grey marble slab top. It is warm, the radiator alive with the hiss of steam and tapping metal sounds.

The greens, golds, whites, and reds of ribbon are colorful snakes that will have to wait for next year to escape. She wraps them around their individual cardboard cylinders and lays them down in a box side by side. Green, Gold, White, and Red.

"Oh, dear, the tags are all mixed up," she said.

"I'm sorry," I said.

The mess was my fault but I didn't want to tell her why. Christmas eve, father had asked me to wrap a special small box, *Would you wrap this for me? It's for your mother, and you always wrap presents much prettier than I can.* And so, I happily wrapped the gift, but I had been in a hurry and left a mess looking for the last tag with a snowman and cheerful birds that carry pretty ribbons in their beaks. Mom loved the ruby pendant so much and she commented on how beautifully he'd wrapped it. Dad winked at me and so it was our little secret that I had wrapped it for him.

The heat of the radiator underneath my hands and elbows. I lean into the warmth. My skinny legs, my pelvis. Even my bones are cold, my chest empty.

Mom picks up the orphaned papers - ones that were cut too small or shaped too awkward to wrap a gift. She flattens them into a neat stack and then rolls them up and puts them in ribbon bag.

"Waste not, want not," she says.

"Mom?"

"Yes dear?"

"Was I...was I a mistake?"

Her hands stop moving. Her brown eyes flat on mine for just a second, then back to the little rectangle tags.

Santas placed with Santas and Candy Canes with Candy Canes.

"Your father and I always wanted four children," she said, "two boys and two girls, and that's what God gave us."

"But why I am *so* much younger than Lydia and George and William Jr.?"

"We had you a few years later," she said, "that's all."

The side of my mom's face, intent on what she is doing. Her hair a soft brown that curled at the bottom and a wave that went across her forehead. A classic beauty, like Katharine Hepburn or Lauren Bacall. My mother didn't smile like pretty women do because she didn't know she was pretty. Decades later after everything bad had settled, she would tell me that her parents always called her the 'smart' one and her sister was the 'pretty' one.

The warmth of the radiator under my palms and fingers. I wanted that warmth to engulf me. The warmth hugged me through the sleeves of my forest green school uniform sweater. The cold hollow ache of my chest pushing up now stuck in my throat. My face got hot, eyes stung.

"I miss Hope," I said.

"I know you do dear."

Mom stacked the name cards into their little cardboard cubbyholes.

Santas with Santas. Waiting till next year.

"But, I'm...I'm sad, really sad," I said.

The ribbons and bows blurred, green, red and gold prisms in my eyes.

"You'll feel better tomorrow," she said, "and next week when you're back in school, you'll be so busy you'll forget they were here."

I wipe my eyes and look out at the snow on the trees. The wide empty boulevard. No one was making snow angels now.

"I don't want to forget," I said quietly.

I wanted more.

More laughter and magical adventures with Little Will.

More of Hope's big arms hugging me. Her laughter. Her comfort.

I wanted more dinosaurs, more snow angels.

I tried to understand what mom said. It didn't make sense to me, but it must be true if she said it: this pain in my chest and heavy sadness would go away once I got back to school.

I stood there too long. Wanting something she couldn't give to me. My toes cold in my shoes. I wished I could put my feet on the radiator too.

"Shouldn't you be reading? Didn't your school assign you a reading list for Christmas break?"

"Yes."

"Well, better hop to it young lady! We don't want to fall behind, do we?"

The paper organized. All the bundles of pretty colors were back in their clear plastic bags and cardboard boxes until next year.

Rolls of paper and boxes in her arms, Mom turned and walked away. I picked up as much as I could off the bay window and radiator and followed her out the bedroom, across the landing by the large stained-glass windows, and up into the pistachio-green staircase to the third floor.

I did not like the third floor there were boogeymen up there. The whole space gave me the creeps. The only time it felt safe was when Little Will was with me, and we would go up there to send secret messages and his stuffed tiger down the laundry chute.

Mom walked into the far back room that would overlook the cherry tree blossoms in April. Now it was covered with snow. Mom bent down slow. Elegant, she never ran her hose. She turned the small latch to open the elf door that went under the eaves, and she put the rolls of paper back there one by one.

Then she stepped aside for me to drop my bundles of ribbons and tags and bows. Of greens, blues, reds and golds.

It was dark and scary under the eaves.

And smelled musty, dusty and dark. I laid the plastic bags down, backed out and mom gently closed the tiny door. The latch snapped shut. There was no latch on the inside.

My stomach clutched again. I hated going up there. I stayed close and followed mom back down the winding green stairway.

Her voice out in front of us, "I'm tired from all the excitement of the last week," she said, "I'm going to lie down for a nap."

She had wanted me to start on my reading homework, but she didn't bring it up again, so I followed her back into the master bedroom.

Mom was tired. She got tired a lot.

She took off her shoes, and with an audible sigh, she laid down on her half of the large four- poster bed. She pulled the crochet throw blanket up over her legs.

I took off my shoes on dad's side of the bed and carefully crawled over to her on my hands and knees slow so as not to disturb her.

She closed her eyes and crossed her hands over her chest like those Egyptian statues we saw pictures of in school. She looked asleep already. Or dead.

I curled-up fetal, perpendicular to her and carefully placed my head on her tummy. She did not object, so I relaxed a bit and listened to her heartbeat slow, soft, distant. Her breath shallow.

Her last rib, the floating rib, moved against the back of my head with each breath. I angled up a bit closer to feel her elbow against my upper back. My feet were still cold, I crossed them and pulled myself up into a ball as small as I could. Shaped and folded like when I was inside her womb.

Comfort in my ear, Mom's stomach sounded like the ocean sounds I would hear when snorkeling with Little Will in the summertime.

Gurgles and waves. Movement through water, food moving through acid. I close my eyes, and I try to fall asleep.

Maybe, just maybe, when I wake-up I won't miss Hope and Little Will so much.

WE ARE

Dad always drank his orange juice first thing in the morning.
Before coffee.
Before cereal.
Standing in his dark gray banker's suit, he surveyed the grassy well-manicured tree-lined boulevard though the big windows of our dining room. The reds and blues of the large thick oriental rug beneath his black, shiny shoes.

He drank his juice in a way that always made a sucking noise through his tight lips. He'd stand there drinking his juice and run his fingers though the loose change in his pocket.

His coins made a quick, sharp, jangly sound. That sound made my chest and gut tighten.

After his juice, he walked back across the dining room, through the swinging door, through the butler's pantry and into the kitchen.

I got our Fiestaware cereal bowls down from the cupboard and placed them across from each other on the kitchen table.

His favorite was orange, mine the pistachio green. He poured Quaker granola into his bowl, then spooned two heaps of sugar over the top with just a bit of milk.

My cereal was a choice between Special K or Grape Nuts with no extra sugar allowed.

"Ready for school today?"

Before I could answer, his eyes drifted past me. He'd chew and chew, crunchcrunchcrunch and rub his napkin between his thumb and forefinger until pieces of it would pill up and fall onto the brown Formica tabletop.

My Special-K got soggy. I poured in too much milk and wasn't eating it fast enough. My stomach hurt again.

Mom was not at the stove, nor in the pantry. There were many mornings since Lydia went to college when mom slept in late.

My dad's blue, blue eyes were sad and far away, although he was just three feet across the table from me.

My ribs clenched in on my stomach.

Third grade, and I was worried.

Jangling change, loud crunchy granola, dad grinding his napkin into powder ran his current of anxiety across the table and into me.

Most days, dad left for work before I left for school, but today he would accompany me on my first time riding the city bus to school. It felt so grown up.

We walked the few blocks to the bus stop in silence. Alone together.

From the bus stop, I could see the large brick colonial. Dense, full hedges hugged the house all around. The corner of the sunroom with her tall windows that opened like French doors where we placed our twelve-foot Christmas tree every year.

But it was spring now, and the maple trees had just popped their bright, first-of-spring-green along the well-manicured boulevard.

It was a privileged childhood for certain, but I absorbed a deep sense of scarcity in that sea of privilege. Many of my classmates already knew they would be given a car of their choice when they turned sixteen and they were already planning what their debutante balls would look like and which boys they would ask to be their escort.

Even in second and third grade it was considered 'normal' for my classmates to safari in Africa and ski the Swiss Alps during the same winter vacation.

That environment of privilege, combined with my parent's childhood trauma and attitudes from the Great Depression and the war, I developed the warped perception that I was poor.

The poorest kid in a rich school and the only one with holes worn through the elbows of her wool uniform sweaters.

I could have a fleet of Mercedes or educated kids, I overheard dad say to his guests over cocktails, *I chose to have educated kids.*

❋ ❋ ❋

Mom and dad were children of the Great

Depression which taught them to value education and be extremely frugal. My mother's father lost everything when the market crashed. He owned a grocery store and allowed many of his customers a line of store credit. When the crash happened, no one could pay, and he lost his business. When my mother and her sister complained about eating oatmeal for weeks on end, my grandmother told her young daughters, *Be grateful your father did not jump out a window and kill himself.* The imprint of fear and abandonment.

My aunt and mother learned to not take anything for granted and never complain. Stoicism. Fear of scarcity was her trauma that shaped her to be frugal and hold all her fears inside. She made work and school top priorities and valued food as nutrition because she knew what it meant to literally go hungry for months. Her father was a veteran of the First World War and started to wake his children every day with marching band music and set them to work. They grew vegetables and stored potatoes and winter squash in their cold cellar. They made jam from summer blackberries and homemade bread, always wheat, never white because wheat had more nutritional value. To make ends meet, they allowed strangers to rent rooms in their house, which led to more trauma for the two young girls who did not have locks on their bedroom doors.

Dad's family was not hit as hard financially during the Great Depression although his trauma was just as deep if not greater. The sudden death of his father by heart attack forced him to become the 'man of the house' at only sixteen and care for his mother.

He fought in Europe after college, and mom served in Washington, DC. After the war, they both worked at the same bank where dad was a manger, and mom a bank teller. They met at a company picnic.

Dad often told the story of their first encounter just as much as mom did, but he emphasized her 'boldness' in telling him off. *One thing about your mother you can count on she's tough and not afraid to speak her mind.*

Dad was the congenial one who got along well with everyone. Their personalities complimented each other well.

※ ※ ※

Now several years and four children later, in the spring of 1974, the baby of the family and her dad waited.

Alone together at the bus stop.

I wore my school uniform skirt with a white Peter Pan collar shirt and my wool uniform blazer. Dad wore one of his grey suits with his grey Stetson hat, and his tan raincoat with the buttons that looked like round tasty caramels.

He held his chestnut-colored leather briefcase in front of him, his large square fingers wrapped around the worn leather handle.

I got his hands - wide paw hands with square boxy fingers. Dad shifted his briefcase to his left side, and with his right hand in his pocket, he ran his fingers through loose change. Moving his coins to make that quick, sharp, jangly sound that went right to my chest and stomach.

Did I remember my bus token?

I reached into the right pocket of my wool uniform blazer. I felt the thin, weightless disk about the size of nickel. I weaved that disk through my fingers inside the dark wool of my jacket pocket the same way dad's worried fingers ran through his change, but my actions were silent.

The front of the bus, a small box in the distance, moved towards us then stopped. Eight or so blocks and only three stops away. Dad punched the air straight out, bent his elbow and looked at his watch.

Finally, the bus reached us.

My father stepped back and I stepped up.

A puff of wind blew the dust up onto my face.

The bus doors folded open. I walked up the three steps. The driver smiled at me. I looked down and dropped my bus token into the change-eater slot.

A seat for two was open on the right about a third of the way back. I sat down and scooted in next to the window. My school uniform skirt went to my knees standing up, but sitting down it didn't cover me.

The seat was cold on the back of my legs. My legs were so skinny that even when I pushed my knees together tight, my green knee socks on my calves barely touched.

Colt legs mom always called them.

Dad dropped his real coins into the slot. A clink and a whirr with each coin dropped in. He turned and walked up the aisle.

As the bus started to move, he reached up and put his hand on the metal railing overhead.

He didn't look at me.

My palm patted the empty seat next to me, I opened my mouth, to say,

"Dad, right here."

I did say it, I think.

Or maybe, I didn't.

Because he did not seem to hear me or see me.

He sat down two rows ahead of me across the aisle.

Right.

There.

Next to an old lady with an orange paisley scarf covering her blue-grey hair.

My face got hot, my feet chilled cold. His salt and pepper hair cropped close, I could see it just below his hat, behind his ear. The angle of his strong square jaw. His eyes looking straight ahead.

At the next stop I pulled my canvas book bag up from the floor in front of me, and sat it on the empty seat next to me.

The empty seat where he should be.

Outside the bus window, I noticed two

people jogging single file along the narrow dirt path that split the boulevard grass in two.

That same single-track path along the boulevard was where dad had taught me to ride my first grown-up bike without training wheels. A green Schwinn Sting-Ray with a banana seat and a flower-trimmed basket on the handlebars.

Sitting on the cold bus seat, my body recalled the somatic memory in my spine. The sensation at the second he let go, when instead of the bike wobbling to the ground as it had several times before, my balance worked and I didn't fall. *That's it, that's it!* his voice and clapping behind me as I rode farther away from him along the narrow dirt path.

Sitting on the bus, a smile came to my face remembering the shared feelings of pure joy and his pride at my simple accomplishment of riding a bike.

I looked over, and he was still just staring straight ahead. On my first city bus ride to school, I was no longer his daughter but just a person riding the same bus.

That tight feeling started again in my chest and stomach. I closed my eyes and began to conjugate the French verbs we had just learned.

My face became hot with shame. I was not good enough for him to sit with or even to acknowledge.

Nerves churned my stomach and fluttered my heart.

I started to conjugate the verb to be.

Je suis, I am.

Tu es, you are.

Il est, he is.

Vous etes…

My school was the next stop. The yellow stucco building behind the field hockey field. I stood up, my eyes straight ahead just like my father, I looked out the big, wide, front windows and walked toward the front of the bus.

My right hand gripped my canvas book bag handle. My books between me and my father.

I walked past him as if he was someone I didn't know. He didn't say anything, and I didn't look back.

The doors opened. I wanted to turn and wave goodbye to him, but I didn't. I stepped down and heard the bus driver say "have a nice day."

In my head I said thanks, but no words came out just a small polite smile. I looked down at my shoes, both my hands on the canvas handle of my book bag, the bus drove on, pushing air up my front.

Air and dust and the bus and my father.

I stood at the crosswalk, the big yellow stucco school in front of me.

Je suis, the cars stopped.

Tu es, I started to cross.

Il est, the stink of car exhaust.

Vous etes. Dirt on yellow stucco.

Curb, sidewalk, the dark tunnel shortcut under the dining hall.

I couldn't remember the rest.

Panic hit my whole body.

I put my book bag down, and grabbed my small, spiral notebook.

My teacher said that notebook was the best for conjugating verbs and learning vocabulary because it had a line down the middle of each page. We'd write French on the left and the English to the right of that narrow maroon line on pistachio-green tinted paper.

Page after page of verbs, nouns. Language. My thumb and index finger pulling up the lower corners of each page.

My lips kept moving as if repeating the ones I remembered would help me remember the ones I forgot.

Je suis,

Tu es,

Il est,

Vous etes, past pages of vocabulary, I looked for my answer.

I'm gonna fail!

Je suis

tu es

il est

vous etes, chest and stomach clenched tight.

Then there it was:

Etre | To Be

My eyes followed the line down the page to the one I missed,

Nous Sommes.

And on the right side of that thin maroon line,

We Are.

SPAGHETTI & BULLIES

By sixth grade I had seen my parents host many elaborate cocktail and dinner parties. Mom would draft a menu and a to-do list specifying everything that needed to occur for a successful party, and she would spend days shopping and preparing the elaborate meals.

She would recruit me to polish the endless sterling silver and help set the table. "Of course you never want to confuse a salad fork with a dessert fork, dear."

Dad would select the wines to pair with

the different courses and sometimes cases of champagne would be ordered.

From a young age, I would be introduced to the guests early in the evening, usually during the cocktails. I would answer their questions about how I liked school, what my favorite subjects were, and where I wanted to go to college. Then it would conclude with the *nice to meet you*, and I would go off to my room. If I was lucky there would be delicious left-overs the next day, but that was rare.

Mother was an excellent cook. Instead of designing bridges and building what civil engineers build, she put her enthusiasm and attention to detail into hosting elaborate parties and well-designed evenings to please her guests and her husband. Their parties were popular not just for the food and drink but also as mom explained to me,

"To be a good hostess you want to make sure that your guests not only enjoy what they eat and drink but also the conversation. And that depends on who you invite. Your father and I like to bring people together from different cliques."

"What is a clique, mom?"

"Well, generally, it's when people who

share similar interests keep company with each other to the exclusion of people with different views or interests. You know how you enjoy sailing with Kim?"

"Yes, of course, I love that!"

I idolized Kim, she was super-smart, graceful and she knew how to win races. Whenever she asked me to crew for her, I dropped everything else. Racing with her was a thrill. She knew how to push the boat and could read the wind and waves and strategize on the fly. She'd yell through the wind to me, "Hike out more and trim the jib, we're gonna catch those guys!" My hands would grip that wet jib sheet as if my life depended on it. Soaking wet leaning out over the salty cold water of Narragansett bay. Wet Top Siders on my bare feet, my ankles hooked under the dirty canvas hiking strap, I would lean back as far as I could and hold. I got stronger, and her confidence in me made me feel more confident in what my body was capable of. She would always thank me when she accepted a win. One time she even gave me the silver plated cup we won, *so you will remember how much fun this was. Never be scared to push yourself and try new things.*

"Well," mom continued, "can you imagine her socializing with you and some of your other friends?"

I imagined it for a second thinking how cool it would be, but then the reality of it hit me: I don't think Kim would be interested in playing Batman and Robin, or Charlie's Angels, that's kid's stuff. So I said,

"Kim is much older, so that would be like Lydia playing superhero with us. It would be kinda weird."

"That's just my point, dear. You are similar to your father and I. You have many interests with friends in different circles that don't necessarily even know of each other."

I thought about the different people I liked being around in addition to Kim:

Trish the RISD student who taught life drawing on Saturday mornings showed me how to really "see" to draw. *You have to look for a long time to see the lights and shadows. Don't draw your idea of a face. Draw what is actually there.*

Or Tammy from summer tennis clinic. We had tea parties at the bottom of her pool and swam like dolphins in the freezing waters off Beavertail Point.

Or Susan who was in my grade, but I did not know her until we both took Mrs. Patterson's dancing class after school on Thursdays. We bonded over our shared suffering of uncomfortable patent leather shoes, white gloves, and the insufferable boys who stepped on our feet and picked their noses. Soon she started sitting with me at school lunch and we talked about Nancy Drew Mysteries.

Then I thought of Miriam and Kathy and Anne and Paige who were exclusive. They did not really associate with other students.

"There are cliques in my class, too."

"I imagine there are."

"But we are all in the same class," I said.

"Well, even in a single grade, there will be girls with different interests."

❋ ❋ ❋

Paige used to be my best friend, but now she only associated with the popular girls who would become debutantes.

From first though fourth grades, Paige and I went to each other's house every other Friday. Sometimes, she would come along as my family's guest for dinner at the University Club. We would get all dressed-up for a formal evening out. At the club, there was a cocktail jazz bar. We would sit at a candlelit table for four with the music of Thelonious Monk or The Glenn Miller Orchestra playing at low volume. Dad would order Shirley Temples for us while he and mom sipped their dry martinis. The four of us would listen to the music, and talk about anything and everything. It felt so grown-up and glamorous. Dad enjoyed talking about Big Band Swing and Jazz. After we finished our drinks, a man wearing a black tailcoat would show us to our table.

Paige was the first friend I had invited to join us for dinner at the University Club, and we would talk about it for days. Sometimes we would go to the school library to find the music we had heard, and play records in the listening booth. We would sing along and memorize our favorites: Paige liked to sing Chet Baker's *My Funny Valentine* and I loved Ella Fitzgerald's *Summertime*.

We liked discovering new foods too. Paige grossed out Susan one Monday during lunch describing the escargot we'd tried that weekend, "Snails smothered in melted butter. We *ate snails*, can you believe it? And they were good!"

Then one Friday, I overheard Paige's mother say to mine, *It's so odd, I found William Sr. and his mother listed in the Social Register, but I could not find you, the boys or Lydia. Can I rightly conclude that your youngest daughter will also not be a debutante?*

I heard my mother's short reply, that I would not be a debutante.

Then Paige stopped coming over.

I was devastated.

Then it got worse.

One Saturday, my parents and I were eating in the formal dining room at the club when I saw Paige and her parents walk in. She waved hello and her mother frowned at her. After they were seated at their table, Paige looked across the dining room at me and smiled. Her mother held up her linen dinner napkin instructing her to put it in her lap.

My mother leaned across the table as discreetly as she could to ask my father, "What are they doing here? They're not members, are they?"

"They are now. Bob asked me if I would recommend him for membership."

Mom sniffed her uppity sniff and said, "And they won't even come over for a proper hello? Typical. New money, no manners."

Mom looked over at me, probably anticipating tears, but I was slowly learning to shut them off before they showed up.

The whole thing was confusing and painful enough but now hearing that my father helped them become members felt like a betrayal. *How could he do that?*

I was not good enough for Paige to be around since I was not going to be a debutante, and yet my father helped them become members of this exclusive club?

Insecurity creeped in with the possibility that my father put Bob's request ahead of my hurt at losing my best friend.

Perhaps he did not know what Paige's mother had said to mom. Perhaps he thought Paige and I were still friends, but it was pretty obvious something was wrong when she did not come over to our table to say hello.

He must not have known about what happened because if he did know, he certainly would put his daughter's well-being ahead of a favor for a man he barely knew. *Wouldn't he?*

Then the guilt followed, what an ungrateful daughter I was to think so poorly of my dad.

The sense of guilt and disbelief caused something else to grow like a teflon shield over my heart. I had to ignore the hurt I felt, or accept the possibility that my father might have valued his relationship with an aquaintance more than his own daughter.

When Paige and I were assigned to get the milk and crackers for morning snack, she would talk and laugh just like when we were best friends, but then when she was around the popular girls, she would ignore me.

※ ※ ※

I tried to picture Kathy and Miriam and Anne and Paige in the same room as me and Joy and Susan.

I had an idea:

"Mom, you said that people enjoy your parties, right?"

"Oh yes, very much."

"Even if they were not friends before?"

"Especially so, your father has been told more than once about new friendships that started at our dinner table."

Feelings of excitement at the idea of having a big successful party that everyone enjoyed, and hopes of being accepted by the popular girls or at least maybe Kathy and Miriam would stop making fun of the holes in my sweaters, and stop sneaking-up on me to stick their wet fingers in my ear when I sit in the front of the class. And maybe if the popular girls accepted me, then maybe Paige and I would be friends again.

"Mom?"

"Yes?"

"Could we, I mean, would you let me have a big party this year for my birthday?"

"How big?"

"I'd like to invite my whole class. You say new friendships are formed at your dinner table, maybe that could happen at my birthday this year."

"Well, parties take a lot of work, the bigger they are the more work to do."

"Please? I can help."

Her hesitation vanished. Then she said,

"We could set up games in the ballroom and open presents in the living room. What would you like to eat?"

"Could we have spaghetti and that really good sauce you make?"

"Grandma's recipe? Well that will take some planning ahead, the sauce has to simmer for at least two days, but certainly. Why not. Spaghetti and meatballs it is!"

Mom grabbed a notepad from under the phone and started to make notes.

"Let's see, if we have twenty plus you that's twenty-one, so....maybe I will bake two or three birthday cakes just to make sure everyone can have seconds if they want to.

"And ice cream?"

"Yes, and ice cream. Balloons and other decorations too," she said, "It will be lovely."

Mom grabbed my hand. I could feel her excitement growing with mine.

"Let's talk it over with your father and see what he thinks. Now don't jump on him right when he walks in the door, let him unwind with his cocktail and newspaper. Then you can bring it up to him at dinner."

At dinner in between bites of broccoli and London Broil glazed with garlic butter I asked dad about my party.

"Inviting all your classmates for your birthday? I think that's a great idea," dad said.

"William, she has twenty classmates. That's quite a few mouths to feed. It will be very expensive."

"Isn't that about the number of people we had at our dinner party last month? You certainly made that a smashing success," dad said, "My boss is still talking about how delicious your chocolate torte was. He wants you to give your recipe to his wife."

They looked at each other in silence.

I looked back and forth like watching a tennis match waiting for a final answer.

Then mom looked at me and said, "Well, dear, your father approves so let's make this your best birthday party yet."

She took a sip of red wine and added,

"I don't think they will all show up, but you are welcome to invite them all."

The next day after school mom took me to Wayland Square to custom order invitations on fancy Crane Paper. Mom made sure they included an 'R.S.V.P.'.

A week later we picked them up and

brought them home. I sat at her desk in the sunroom behind the wall of tall succulent plants, and personalized each invitation trying to make my cursive writing as neat and pretty as possible. The following afternoon mom helped me lick all twenty envelopes.

At school I asked Ms. Edelhurst permission to hand them out, and when would be a good time to do so. Handing them out to each student, I explained it was for my birthday party and how nice it would be if they could make it.

Mom and I worked together on the menu and by the time my birthday arrived the following month, I was so focused on how to please everyone who would attend, that I almost forgot that the party was for my birthday.

I was so excited to show Anne and the popular girls my house and so hoped they would have a good time. They all RSVP'd *yes*, so they were all coming!

My deep roiling anxiety mixed with anticipation and my desire to host the best party ever was tempered only by mom keeping me busy with various tasks like stirring the meat sauce every hour for one whole Saturday, inflating the balloons, helping set the table, and folding twenty-one linen napkins into a fancy ring shape to stand on each place setting.

When everyone arrived, we played games in the basement before lunch, and then Anne said, "Show us the rest of your house!"

"Yeah," Kathy said.

Mom said, "I will stay here with any girls who would like to continue the games or play ping pong."

About half the girls followed me upstairs to my bedroom. They wandered around looking at my books and things.

Kathy and Miriam walked over to my bed and touched my stuffed animals and Miriam said to Kathy, "She has no dolls."

The room fell silent, then Kathy said,

"Why don't you have any dolls? It's such a girly room all pink and white, but... no dolls?"

"That's kinda weird," Miriam said.

They both looked at me for an explanation.

"I dunno," I said, "Grammy gives me stuffed animals each Christmas and Easter and sometimes just because she wants to."

I loved my stuffed animals which were mostly all Steiff brand partly because they looked so real and mostly because Grammy gave them to me and I loved her very much.

I thought of my friend Brenda who I swam and sailed with in summer. She had Ken and Barbie dolls and we would play with them and dress them in different outfits, but I never asked for dolls of my own. I liked my stuffed animals.

Kathy picked-up one from my window sill and laughed holding it up for everyone to see,

"Oh I remember this one - you brought it to school for show and tell."

A giggle went like a wave through my room, and all eyes were on Kathy holding my parakeet up in the air.

"Show and tell? Show what? It's a stuffed parakeet," Anne said.

I felt my face getting hot, and then even hotter at the awareness that it likely showed.

Kathy continued, "It was so funny. In third grade we had show and tell, and she brought it to school in a real cage with birdseed and newspaper and everything."

I remembered that day. I wanted to defend

my actions, but the real story would only sound more pathetic, and bring the risk of tears.

What they didn't know, was that I had a real parakeet I planned to bring for show and tell, but he died two days before. I substituted my Steiff parakeet that Grammy had given me. It looked quite real, and I had told the class, "He's not real," but then pretended he was to show how to feed him, change his water, remove the tray and clean his cage. I got high marks from the teacher, but Kathy made fun of me for days, coming up to me at lunch and saying things like, "Does he sing to you? Does he poop? Do you imagine that too?" Then she and Miriam would walk away laughing.

My friend Joy saw my growing embarrassment, and interrupted the laughter with, "Let's see the rest of the house."

Walking down the hallway from my bedroom, Anne stopped when she noticed the two doors in the wall.

"What are these?" She asked.

I opened the smaller door, "This is a laundry chute."

"I have those at my house too," Miriam said

to Anne, "I've shown you."

Anne nodded to Miriam and then said to me,

"Can I look?"

"Sure," I said.

She put her head into the dark vertical tunnel that smelled of cedar wood, and looked down.

"I can't see anything. Does it go all the way to the basement?"

"Yes, if I had a flashlight you would likely see my dad's shirts at the bottom."

"Pretty cool huh?" Joy said.

Joy and I used to drop stuffed animals and notes down there like Little Will and I did when playing our spy games.

"And it's for laundry," Diane asked, "How does that work?"

As I was explaining to Diane, Anne pointed to the larger door next to the laundry chute and asked,

"And what's that one?"

"This," I said opening the door, "is a dumb waiter."

Her eyes got wide as she looked at the two dusty wooden shelves and dry darkened-with-age ropes.

"Do you use it?"

"Not really," I said.

Joy glanced over at me with a quick smile. I knew we were both thinking of the time we got caught using it to sneak Ritz crackers with cheddar cheese up to the second floor. The top shelf and ropes were so dusty-dry that there was dust on the cheese when it got to us; and the old metal pully system made enough noise going up the shaft that mom had heard it and caught us. But we did not share that with the group.

Instead I said, "I mean, it has been used, but it's not supposed to be."

"Could I get on it?" Anne asked.

"It's not for people," I explained. "It's an elevator for food and things."

Anne looked at Miriam and Kathy and said, "I bet somebody really small could fit in there."

"Yeah," Kathy said, "Someone small and light, like Maggie. Maggie where are you?"

Maggie was quietly talking with Susan under the tall stained-glass windows on the landing between the first and second staircase.

"Maggie, come see this," Miriam called to

her.

She slowly walked up the four stairs to the second landing with extra effort to go as fast as her braces would let her.

"It's not for people," I said again.

"Oh come on, this will be fun," Kathy said.

"Maggie, do you want to go for a ride?" Miriam asked.

"What is it?" Maggie asked pushing her glasses up the bridge of her nose.

"It's a small elevator," Anne said, "c'mon get in, we can give you a ride downstairs so you don't have to walk."

Maggie moved closer, her shoulders rounded in more than usual.

Fear and anger started to well up in my gut.

* * *

I flashed on my much older brother George, the sound of his laugh, the look on his face when he would ask me if I wanted to play *fifty-two card pick-up*. It was always the same: his laugh as cards flew everywhere, followed by his command, *now get down on your hands and knees and pick them up. And count. Each one. Out loud.*

After I picked them up, he would insist he count them himself. *If any are missing you know mom and dad will be very upset. These are the ones they use to play bridge with the Jamisons.*

He would make me stand there and watch as he slowly counted each one, sometimes he would sneak one in his pocket or hold two together to torment me, *You missed one. Get down and look for it or we can start over if you want to.*

I realized the only way to stop his game was to hide the cards. So I took them and hid them in my sock drawer.

That night George decided to try something else. I forgot to put the cards back in Dad's desk drawer.

The following Saturday when the Jamison's came over for cocktails and bridge, mom came in without knocking and said,

"George told me you were playing with your father's cards. Where are they?"

I sheepishly took them out of my bureau behind my socks and handed them to mother.

"You know these are your father's cards

and not for you to play with. Why did you take them when we told you not to?"

I told her about George and his game of fifty-two card pick up. She looked at me for a long time and then she said,

"Don't you ever lie to me young lady. Your brother would never do such a thing."

She grabbed my arm and took me across the hall to my bathroom and placed me next to the sink. Turned on the tap, and lathered the bar of Ivory Soap between her hands.

"We are going to wash your mouth out with soap young lady so you will learn not to lie," and she jammed her hand in my mouth.

The initial shock, gagging on the taste of the soap, her fingers hitting the back of my throat.

"Don't ever lie to me again. Never. Ever."

I stared at my blue Disney mug with Goofy on it and the tube of Ultra Brite toothpaste.

My mouth was no longer mine.

❊ ❊ ❊

"It's not strong enough to hold a person," I said, "it's very old and the ropes are frayed."

Anne looked at me straight in the eye and

held me in a stare that seemed an eternity. I thought of how Mom had told me to never get in there myself or allow anyone else to be in there. *It's made for casseroles not people. Don't ever crawl in there. You hear me? It will break, fall fifty feet to the basement and you will get hurt very badly.*

Mom was still in the down in the ballroom. I had asked her to let me show my guests around alone in hopes that I would impress them, but now I wished that she would magically appear at the top of the stairs. I often wished she would appear when George babysat me too, but I was on my own, and as usual, the house was too big for her to hear me even when I did call for help.

Finally with her eyes still on mine, Anne said, "Maggie, do you want to go for a ride?"

"Ok," Maggie said.

"We can't do that," I said, "my mother told me that people are never to get on this."

"Do you always do what your mummy tells you," Miriam asked.

Joy jumped in to help, "She's right, her mom told us it's forbidden."

"Ooooo, forbidden," Miriam said smiling at Kathy.

The two of them grinning behind Anne. Maggie stood next to Anne now, looking smaller than ever. Anne looked over at Maggie, and then back at me. I had seen that face before.

Anne said with a curled lip,

"You are such a chicken. Most boring birthday party ever."

"Yeah you're being a big baby," Miriam said.

Kathy laughed and said loud enough for all the girls standing around to hear,

"Did you see all those stuffed animals she has on her bed?"

"And no dolls," Anne said, "what girl doesn't have any dolls?"

The three of them turned away, and started to walk down the stairs.

My heart racing, the palm of my right hand flat against the closed door of the dumb waiter. I looked at Maggie and said quietly, "I am so sorry."

She smiled a half-smile, turned and started to walk toward the stairs far behind the other girls.

I watched her walk away. Her green knee-socks between those metal rails.

I hated myself for what had just happened.

I should have been mad at Anne, Miriam and Kathy, but I wasn't.

Instead, I turned it all on myself, imagining what mom would say if I told her:

What did you do to make them do that?

Or she might say,

Well young lady, that's what you get for wanting to show them the house yourself. You should have let me do it.

* * *

The dining room table was beautiful. Mom had tied colorful balloons to the chandelier and placed vases of fresh flowers at each end of the oak sideboard. She had accented the table with strategically placed bright Fiestaware bowls brimming with salted cashews and macademia nuts. The sunlight was streaming in the dining room windows. It was perfect.

Anne, Miriam, Kathy and Paige sat next to each other to my left and Joy, Susan, Diane, and Maggie sat to my right. Mom added extra leaves to the oak table so it made a long oval with comfortable spacing for twenty guests and me. I sat in Dad's chair at the head of the table.

Mom served fancy Waldorf salads first and then the spaghetti and meatballs with fresh garlic bread. She brought each girl a plate and our cleaning lady, Patrice, stayed-on to help.

About half-way through our spaghetti course, Anne suggested we play the game of telephone, "It's where someone whispers something to a person and it goes around the table until the last person says it out loud and you see how much it changed or stayed the same."

"Ok," I said, "I can start."

"Usually," Miriam said, "it ends with the guest of honor, so you would go last."

I had never played it before, and was happy that the popular girls were engaging in my party. Just like mom said, people who didn't really know each other were connecting at my parent's table. Despite what had happened in the hallway upstairs, I was still hopeful for new friendships forming and for everyone to have a good time.

Anne looked at Joy sitting directly to my right and said, "Joy why don't you start?"

Joy thought for a second and then covering her mouth, she whispered something into Susan's ear.

And so it went, each girl hearing the phrase and passing it all around the table.

Finally, Kathy sitting next to me, leaned over and whispered in my ear,

"The spaghetti is hard."

"What? Say that again?"

She leaned in again, her voice with an edge to it, she said,

"The. Spa-geh-tee. Is. Hard."

I sat up taller trying to see if people had eaten their spaghetti. *How awful*.

Anne looked at me and said,

"Well, what was the phrase? You have to say it out loud, and then the person who started it tells what it was at the beginning."

I swallowed and said, "The spaghetti is hard?"

"What was it?" Miriam said, grinning.

I repeated myself, "The spaghetti is hard."

"Wait," Joy said, "that's not what I said."

"What did you say, Joy?" Kathy asked.

Joy was turning red, "I said, 'I forgot to bring a card'."

She looked at me, "Really, it's on the kitchen table at my mom's."

My face hot again and my words stuck in

my throat, "That's ok, Joy."

"I am so sorry for anyone whose spaghetti wasn't cooked all the way. Does anyone want more spaghetti," I tried to make light of it, "hopefully softer this time?"

I noticed most of the plates were wiped clean including Anne's. A murmur went around the table, and I so wished I could control my blush, it always gave me away.

Anne, Miriam and Kathy were giggling among themselves. Paige was looking down at her lap, not laughing. I wondered why she was friends with them, but then again, I had wanted to be too.

Joy read my expression of *what now?*

"I will go tell your mother we are ready for the cake," she said, and headed into the pantry.

❊ ❊ ❊

After the everyone left, mom sent Patrice home, and I helped in the kitchen, drying dishes and forks and spoons and glasses as she washed them all by hand.

"Well that was a success," she said.

"Not exactly," I said, and I told her what

they said about the spaghetti being hard.

"Serving twenty-one plates of hot spaghetti is not easy," mom said, "to cook it all at the same time and have it just right."

I thought about dinners she had made for just as many people that seemed more complicated to me, but she had gone to a lot of trouble and I did not want to be ungrateful.

I didn't tell mom about the dumb waiter. I felt terrible about how they treated Maggie. I never should have let it get that far. I had wanted so desperately to impress Anne, Miriam and Kathy. Why had I wanted so much to impress them?

As for the spaghetti being undercooked, either they made it up, which would be mean. Or it was true. Either way, my birthday party did not go as I had hoped it would. I so wanted it to be a success like mom and dad's dinner parties.

❊ ❊ ❊

The following Monday at school, Joy gave me my birthday card that she had forgotten to bring to the party. It was a huge card and very silly. She signed it *Your Friend Always,*

Robin. I thanked her for being so helpful at the party. She smiled her broadest of smiles and said, "Anytime, Batman."

* * *

At gym before kickball started, I noticed Anne, Miriam and Kathy standing around Maggie, and Anne was swatting the pom-pom on Maggie's hat like a cat messing with a mouse.

Walking closer, I heard them taunt her, "Would you have gotten on that dumb waiter, huh? Or are you chicken too, four-eyes."

Not only did Maggie have to wear braces on both legs, but wore thick glasses, and they looked like they might grab for those too.

I found my voice,

"Hey!"

I stepped in between them and Maggie.

My body acted on instinct,

"If you want to hurt her, you have to go through me."

Our gym teacher was not there yet and when my brain caught up to my body, I remembered it was not smart to be confrontational, it could get bad very fast.

My heart was in my throat and I felt my chest and stomach tighten.

Kathy took one step closer to me and said,

"What are you going to do, send your attack parakeet after us?"

They all laughed hard.

"Leave Maggie alone," I said.

In that moment, my body knew I would defend her no matter what they tried.

"This is a waste of time," Anne said, "Let's leave the baby and four-eyes alone, you're perfect for each other."

The three of them walked over to Paige who had been watching us from a distance. She looked at me, then turned and walked away with them.

During kickball in gym that day, my unused adrenalin went into the ball and I kicked it hard towards mid-field. Anne caught it for a second with an audible "oomph", then dropped it, and I ran safely to third base. I could see Maggie on the sidelines, all glasses and smile.

* * *

After school that day, I started walking home when a blue Saab pulled over a few feet ahead of me, and the passenger window rolled down. I recognized it as the same car that dropped Maggie at school. Her mother leaned over towards the passenger window and invited me to come over that Friday.

"Yes, thank you, that sounds fun," I said.

"Our house is not as big as yours, but Maggie has lots of games to play. Would you like a lift? Your house is on the way, it's no trouble."

Once I was in the car, Maggie asked me, "Have you ever played Battleship?"

Thus began a new friendship. I became her bodyguard when she needed one and every other Friday afternoon I went to her house with a book and some Toll House cookies.

Maggie had more toys than I'd ever seen. We played chess, drew on her Etch-A-Sketch, took turns reading Hardy Boys and Nancy Drew books aloud, and she always won whenever we played chess or Battleship.

One day, she handed me her Lite-Brite and said,

"Show me what your parakeet looked like."

As I placed the yellow and green plastic pegs into the holes, they pierced the construction paper and filled with light. The shape of a bird with the greens and yellows of a parakeet began to appear, I started to tear up.

"It's silly, it was so long ago," I said, feeling embarrassed.

"That's ok," she said, "I understand, my dog got out of the yard, and was hit by a car when I was eight. I still miss him a ton."

"What was your dog's name," I asked.

"Max!"

"Was he big?"

Maggie smiled, "No, he was a tiny dog, fluffy and very small. My mom said the first time I saw him I pointed and said, "Max!" so that became his name. What was your parakeet's name?"

"Star," I said, "she loved to sit on my shoulder."

Maggie told me all about her adventures with Max and how much he enjoyed chasing frisbees and chewing her dad's shoes.

Later that afternoon, over mugs of hot cocoa, Maggie said,

"I wonder if they are friends up in heaven?"

We decided, somewhere up there wherever beloved pets go, a sensitive parakeet and a tough Pomeranian were the best of friends.

MIDOL &
TIGER BEAT

My sister Lydia scheduled her wedding for my thirteenth birthday. "That way we will always remember the date," she said, "and my birthday present to you is that you will be my Maid of Honor."

She was engaged to a man named Eric, a Russian Studies graduate student she met during summer term. Lydia asked to wear our mother's wedding dress.

Mom had stored it carefully, tucked away, and when we opened the box we saw that it had aged beautifully. What was once pure white satin with a pearl inlay bodice and a modest train was now a beautiful, soft golden-ivory color.

I wondered if I too would be able to wear my mother's wedding dress someday, but was afraid to ask the question. Somehow I knew I would never wear that particular dress.

Lydia and my mother were in the master bedroom in front of the full-length mirror. She was telling mom the story again, and I never got tired of hearing it. Eric was into health and fitness, a runner, and one day when she was late leaving for class she saw him for the first time.

"I just knew," she said, "as he was jogging towards me, I had this feeling, this knowing-feeling in my whole body: *That's the man I will marry*. When I looked back, he was looking back at me."

"Please keep your arms up and hold still, Lydia," mom said.

My sister held her arms straight out not moving while mother placed pins along the seams around her upper torso and under the arms.

I sat cross-legged on the floor off to the side becoming the third point of a narrow triangle between them and the mirror.

My sister was talking excitedly about her future husband and all his plans after he finished graduate school, "His Russian is flawless and so many recruiters have been seeking him out. If he gets the job he wants with the State Department, he said we would live in Virginia."

She breathed shallow so as not to move the pins or get stuck by one near her armpit. She took three quick breaths and said, "And if we do live in Virginia, I would be able to ride horses again!"

Lydia was a competitive equestrian. The blue ribbons still lined the walls above the picture moulding in her room. I liked to sit on her bed and count them. Thirty-six blue ribbons with gold lettering. She gave me one of her old riding jackets before she left for her year in France. It was too big for me, but I loved to wear it when Little Will and I were on our covert missions in East Berlin.

"How cool would it be if Eric became a real spy," I said. Lydia smiled.

My industrious mother was focused on

the task at hand. My grandmother was a wonderful dressmaker out of necessity, and she taught my mom and my aunt excellent dressmaking and sewing skills in the years before the war. Mom was so frugal that she would darn my father's socks when they got a hole rather than buying a new pair.

I started to feel cramps in my stomach. I thought I might be getting sick or just my anxious tummy. I went into my mother's bathroom and when I pulled down my underwear, a wave of panic went through me at seeing two dark spots in the cotton crotch.

"I'm bleeding!"

I heard my sister laughing.

Mom without missing a beat calmly said,

"You started your period. You'll find a belt and napkins in the cabinet next to the sink."

I knew what a period was, but I wasn't ready to start it now, less than a week before my sister's wedding?

With my underwear around my knees, I waddled over to the cupboard, and pulled out the pad and belt. I assembled this hideous contraption consisting of a thick long pad that I pulled the front and back ends through what looked like an ugly bigger version of my mother's garter belts.

The pad was thick and bulky and the elastic belt around my waist rough against my skin. I wiped off the small bit of blood, and pulled up my underwear positioning everything best I could. I smoothed my school uniform skirt down over my underwear and thighs. The pad was too long and the ends of it formed visible bumps in the front and back of my skirt.

It was horrifying to think of going to school with that. Everyone would be sure to notice it. I feared I would be teased mercilessly.

I had wanted for so long to grow up to be like my sister and Hope, and now I wondered, was this what it meant to be a woman?

I washed my hands and walked back to where I had been sitting. Ugh. It felt like I had a towel bunched up between my legs when I walked. I sat down carefully as to not move anything out of place.

"You, got, your peer-eee-ood," my sister teased in her taunting sing-songy voice.

"Lydia, that's enough," mom said, and she looked over at me for a second, "find everything alright?"

"Ouch!" Lydia said.

"Well don't move. And stop teasing your sister," mom said.

Mom with a pin between her lips said, "We'll get you some sanitary pads and your own belt tomorrow."

I went into my dad's den to call my best friend from school to share the news. Joy was what mom called an *early bloomer*. She was already wearing bras and had started her period the year before.

"That's great," she said cheerfully, "but you really should get tampons. They are less messy and much more comfortable once you get used to them."

I got lightheaded and had a sudden wave of pain along with the sensation that my insides were going to drop to the floor.

"I gotta go," I said and hung up.

I walked slow down the stairs and laid down on the couch hoping for the pain to pass.

My father folded his newspaper and pulled off his reading glasses.

"What's the matter? Are you not feeling well?"

"Woman stuff, Dad. I got my…it hurts real bad."

I could feel the tears coming up.

Why am I such a baby?

"Where's your mother?"

"She's upstairs with Lydia, taking-in the dress a bit."

Dad sat his paper down, came over to me and pulled the throw blanket down from the back of the couch. He covered me and pulled it up to just under my chin and then smoothed my hair back off my face.

"Try to rest. I will be back in a little bit."

About a half hour later, dad was standing next to me with a brown paper bag in one hand and a glass of ginger ale in the other.

He set the glass down on the coffee table coaster and handed me the paper bag.

"Here, this might help you feel better," he said.

Inside there was a bottle of Midol and the latest copy of Tiger Beat magazine with Sean Cassidy and Leif Garrett on the cover. My surprize at what he had done for me came out in a squeak, "Thank you, daddy!"

He walked back to his chair and continued reading his newspaper.

The two Midol went down almost too easy with the ginger ale. I laid back down under the blanket waiting for the knifing pains to subside. If this was how much it hurt to have a period, how much more painful would it be to have a baby? The thought of that scared me.

I opened the magazine to distract myself from the sharp pains and then the cramps stopped just as abruptly as they had started. The Midol worked like magic!

With the pain gone, my whole body started to relax. I felt so safe there on the couch with my dad a few feet away reading in his chair.

He had brought me comfort and showed me a nurturing side of himself that I had not seen before.

When I was little he taught me important things like how to tie my shoes, how to swim, and ride a bike. In the last few years it had been more about grades and how I was doing in school.

I thought of the way Hope had described my father to me years before, *he was kind and supportive...Your father was wonderful to us.*

My mom upstairs with Lydia preparing her dress for the big day most girls dream about, and I was content being near my dad who saw me without judgment, and helped the pain go away.

FOUND & LOST

The summer I turned 14 was the first year I had a job away from home. I was going to be a live-in nanny, helping my brother William and his wife Hope care for their sons Little Will and Benji.

I had held odd jobs cutting grass, babysitting and pulling weeds in my grandfather's huge garden the summers before that, but this was a fancy job, a real job, with weekly pay and everything. Hope, had talked with my mom about it, and when I asked if I could go, mom had sniffed her uppity sniff and said,

"That's fine. But she is paying you way too

much money." I was thrilled she agreed to let me go. I felt so grown up, I could almost forget my mother's disapproving tone. Almost.

* * *

The movie Jaws was one of the big summer blockbusters a few summers before and Hope had given me the paperback book to read. She loved to talk about sharks - especially when we were swimming.

One Saturday during that amazing month of July we were all at the beach and my brother offered to watch the boys while Hope and I went out for a swim alone.

Hope was a strong swimmer, and after we got several feet away from shore, we were treading water in ten feet of clear Cape Cod blue, when she asked "Should we swim out to the raft today?"

It was high tide, and the raft was at least another twenty yards out in what seemed much deeper water. There were several people on it, dancing around, jumping off the diving board, pulling up on the ladder and leaping out for another turn.

"No this is fine," I said.

Salt water dripped from her short, light brown, wiry hair onto her thick tan shoulders. Her eyes a deep heather blue. I wanted to be a grown-up like her, beautiful like her.

She started laughing at me, "You're scared."

"No. No, I'm not."

My heart was racing. I tried to hide it.

I was treading water and watching the people on the raft. Maybe I should swim out there, but I don't know them.

One tall, blond boy wearing light blue swim trunks looked so happy. "Cannonball!" he shouted out then launched himself off the diving board two feet up and out, knees to chest making a huge splash. People on the raft whooped and hollered.

Sharks are attracted to loud noise and movement.

"Duh-nuh, duh-nuh." Hope grabbed my left thigh. I screamed. I turned around, and there she was - laughing her round full laugh that was pure joy.

A small bit of pee escaped from my green one-piece Speedo bathing suit.

"That's not funny." I said coughing up salt

water.

I swam a few feet away and dove down below, reaching though the clear water for the sandy bottom. I always felt more comfortable and fearless underwater because I could see what was below. My body moved easily though the water. I imagined I was a dolphin or a mermaid. I was lithe, longer and more flexible than last summer.

* * *

My father taught me how to swim at the age of four in the dark, cold waters of Narragansett Bay. He would stand on the steps on one side of the dock up to his waist in the water at high tide. I would stand on the parallel set of steps on the other side of the dock.

Even though it was a bright sunny day, the water underneath the dock between those two stairs was in shadow, so I could not see into the water. He was less than ten feet away, but the space of black water underneath the dock between me and him seemed a gulf too far.

His arms reaching out he said, "Just come to me. I'll catch you."

Finally, I splashed over to him wildly in the brisk cold water attempting my first dog paddle.

"That's it!" His big smile and open arms made me feel triumphant.

By seven years old I was a strong swimmer, but still fearful of swimming in deep dark water. It wasn't until I started snorkeling and could see beneath the surface that the underwater world became my comfort zone.

* * *

Now swimming with Hope at the Cape, I was eyes-open underwater with no sharks in sight. Treading water Hope's thick legs moved slowly. The green and white flowered pattern of her bathing suit shimmered underwater. She wore the same style as my mom complete with a modest skirt.

Coming up for air, the weight of my water-soaked hair tugged at my scalp.

Water-bubble sounds of Hope humming the "Jaws" theme and her laughter chased me all the way back into shore.

The sand was so dry it squeaked with every step. My brother and the boys had a huge sandcastle under construction. Little Will carried buckets of sea water to fill the large moat while his younger brother, Benji, shaped the wet sand into towers using his mold and shovel so carefully.

"And what's the part of the castle where the arrows are shot from?" my brother asked his sons.

"The turret!"

"Turret, that's right Benji. Good job!"

I stepped to the other side of the chairs and snuggled down into the warmth of my towel on the hot sand. The salt water evaporated quickly tightening my skin and tickling my ears.

Sun warmed the back of my legs, shoulders and side of my face. Hope sat in her low beach chair. Slow falling droplets of seawater darkened the dry sand below her chair.

"Anyone ready for lunch?" Hope asked.

"Yes, thank you" we almost all said in unison. Eyes closed. The hollow sound of her lifting off the Igloo cooler lid.

"OK, come on over," Hope said.

I could feel the energy of Little Will and Benji running over. The rumble of ice. The crinkly sound of waxed paper wrapped sandwiches.

"We have Tuna, ham or PB and J."

"Peanut butter, please," Little Will said.

"For me too mommy," Benji always copied his older brother whom he adored.

"Ham sounds good to me," my brother said.

My stomach growled. I dug my toes deeper into the hot sand. Eyes closed, I did not want to move, the happiness and sense of belonging on that perfect day was magical. I wanted to soak it all in to imprint it into my whole body and keep it forever.

I felt Benji's small sandy foot on the back of my calf. "Aunt Beth, are you going to have a sandwich?"

Mom never allowed us to eat lying down.
Sit up and eat like a lady.

I turned over and sat up, "Yes, I would love a tuna sandwich, please."

"Here you go." Hope said.

Benji jumped in between us, "I do it."

And with both his hands he took the waxed paper wrapped sandwich from her tanned hand and carried it with both his hands over to me only a couple feet away.

"Thank you Benjamin, that is very kind of

you!" I said.

And with his peanut butter and jelly sandwich in his hands, he skipped back over to his father and sat down next to him.

I watched as Hope took more things from the cooler. Her fingers were long and tanned. I wished for elegant hands like that instead of the square-fingered ones I got from my Dad. Her gold wedding band sparkled with a single drop of salt-water that caught the sunlight.

Hope taught me how to make sandwiches that summer: rich, thick tuna fish sandwiches with tomato and thin slices of celery on Pepperidge Farm bread and just the right amount of mayo.

Mom didn't approve of what Hope prepared for meals. Ever since Benji told her last summer about how much he liked marshmallow and peanut butter sandwiches and declared that peas came from a can, not from grandpa's garden, well mom was horrified.

I was still hungry and wanted to have a second sandwich, but could hear mom's voice in my mind, *why anyone would prefer store bought bread to homemade is beyond me.*

I asked for a diet Tab soda instead.

Two hours later after sand castle empires were built and destroyed, and treasures were found from walking the beach and snorkeling in the waves, it was time to head home.

"Shotgun!" I called out. I broke into a sprint, ran up behind Little Will, and tapped him on his shoulder as I passed him. His legs reached in their wet nylon-swim shorts behind me. My hand reached the door first.

"Not fair! You have longer legs!" Little Will tumbled into the car with his towel, bucket, mask, snorkel and nylon mesh diver's bag.

Just like our imaginary games we made up at Christmas time, pretending to be dinosaurs or spies, in the summer we hunted for treasure and sharks!

That day Little Will's dive bag carried his treasures of green sea glass and sand dollars. It was a good day.

As we pulled up the house, Hope's brother Larry was hosing down a row of bluefish he caught that day.

"Go ahead and get showered right away," Hope said.

My brother was already out of the car and walked directly to the cooler and took out a beer, deftly popping the can open and taking his first long draw with one hand.

Larry turned the hose on me Little Will and Benji, making us sprint from the hot car to the outdoor shower. After rinsing the sand off us under cold-cold water, we headed inside.

Still in my bathing suit and with my towel snug around my waist, I went into the kitchen. Ocean swimming, sun and snorkeling always made me hungry.

I rinsed off a peach from the fruit bowl on the counter and started to devour it. The sweetness could not fill my mouth fast enough.

Peach juice dripped down my chin and into the brushed steel sink.

I could see my brother and Larry through the kitchen sink window reviewing the catch of the day. A line of bluefish laid out on the grass. I counted eight - each one must have been two or three feet long like small sharks all silvery blue-gray, reflecting the sun.

The men were preparing to gut the fish and fillet them. Two would be for dinner, and then they would ceremoniously prep the rest for the freezer. I opened the window, and their voices came in on the warm breeze.

"Are you heading out again tomorrow?"

"Sure," Larry said, "when they're running like this, you gotta get as much as you can, while you can."

"Good, I will join you. Maybe I can do some spear fishing off the boat too," my brother said.

I wiped the juice off my chin and reached for another peach. The peach fuzz smoothed under the water pressure from the tap. Drying salt water started to tickle inside my ears. My skin felt tight. I was getting darker each day. I wanted to be a beautiful dark golden brown like Hope.

In the summers when I was outside all the time, dad would call me his "little brown berry." I loved it when he called me that. I missed dad, but not so much mom.

I could hear her critical voice as if she were standing right there in the kitchen with me:

"Don't eat standing up, it's bad for your digestion.

"Don't eat between meals, you'll ruin your appetite."

"You're having another one??"

I knew how her eyes would settle on my

waist while she talked. My stomach muscles tightened standing over the sink feeling the sting of her words even though she was miles away.

Mom would always tell me I had colt legs when I was younger, but once I turned thirteen, she was certain I was getting fat. I wasn't, but I started to feel fat from the inside.

Larry held up a bluefish by its gills and inserted the buck knife right below the head, and sliced down the white belly to its tail.

He lifted one side grabbed the insides swept them out into the bucket.

Little Will called to me from upstairs, "Ok. I'm done!"

I looked at the remaining part of the delicious peach in my hand. I squeezed it hard until I felt the sharp tip of the pit poke into my palm. Juice and peach pulp oozed between my fingers and down the inside of my wrist. I threw it away and rinsed my hands.

Heading upstairs, I slowed to look closer at the numerous family pictures in the foyer and all along the wall up the stairs. I was not used to seeing so many pictures around. It was very different from how my parents decorated, and I liked it.

There was only one photograph hung on the many walls of my parent's house. It was a large, gold-framed candid shot of William Jr., Lydia and George, all dressed-up and laughing. The image of it was burned in my mind and I recalled it going up the stairs. William Jr. had his mouth open at the beginning of a smile, as if he had just told a joke or heard one and was starting to laugh. George was in profile smiling looking over at William Jr., and Lydia was in the middle looking at the camera with a smile that showed she thought it funny too. It was taken outside in front of a large fancy tent. It may have been William Jr. and Hope's wedding.

That photo of my much older siblings was centered above the living room couch, prominently placed for all guests to see. They all looked happy, beautiful and perfectly photogenic like models or French film stars.

In that moment walking up the stairs of the Cape Cod house that afternoon, looking at the black and white framed photos of Hope's extended family and ancestors next to new color photos of her and William Jr. and the boys, the contrast hit me. Hope's entire family history was displayed, but my parents had only the one photo of my siblings framed and hung in the living room. In our huge, cold, cavernous house, that was the only photo. There were no images of me.

Invisible.

"Can we play badminton before dinner?" Little Will asked me from the top of the stairs.

"Let's see if we have time, buddy," I said.

"Me too, me too," Benji shouted. The door to the boy's room was open and Hope was pulling a shirt over Benji's head.

"Can I help you with dinner prep?" I asked her.

"Sure, how about a big salad? And there's time to play a little badminton with the boys after you take your shower," Hope said.

"Yay! Yay!" Benji jumped up and down. "Bat-mitten!" He was such a happy boy always singing and dancing.

"Hold still," Hope said, let's get your shorts on right young man, one leg at a time."

* * *

After my shower, I didn't want to get

dressed. Nothing felt right. Even the soft, plush towel was too much. I started to pat myself dry, then gave up, and decided to let the water evaporate off me.

My skin was so sensitive, not burned, but spilling over with the warm sunlight of that perfect day. Fine hairs stood up straight on my arms. Anything other than air was too much. With my back and shoulders still wet, I put on my bra. The straps felt uncomfortable, but I was now showing too much to go without one.

My body was changing every day. Some days I longed for the time when I didn't have to wear a bra at all, and sometimes I loved that I was finally getting breasts like my sister.

I pulled on my track shorts with my favorite powder blue Lacoste shirt. Raising up my shoulders, the shirt stuck to my damp skin.

I pulled my long damp un-brushed hair back from my face with two barrettes, and headed downstairs toward the smell of fresh cut grass, and the sound of my brother's voice.

The front door was open and everyone was out on the lawn.

"Stand back, boys. Daddys got a knife."

William Jr. slit open a bluefish gills to tail in one swift motion. More pink guts slooped out into the tan plastic bucket.

Little Will ran over to me swinging his badminton racquet.

"Is that your sword, Prince Caspian?"

"Yes!" he said.

And Benji was right behind him swinging a badminton racquet that was almost as tall as he was.

I walked to the far side of the lawn. The badminton net was always up that summer. It divided the front lawn into two large areas of soft grassy green.

The whistling birdie only had time to go back and forth over the net for a few hits when Hope called out to me from the front door,

"Your Mom's on the phone."

"I'll be right back," I yelled over the net to my nephews, set my badminton racquet down, and headed back toward the house. The grass was so soft and warm under my bare feet.

Going from the hot sun into the hallway my skin puckered with goose bumps. The black and white tiles of the front hall were cool. I picked up the receiver from the front hall table.

"Hi Mom!" I said a little out of breath and smiling.

"Hello," she said, "are you having a good time with your brother?"

"Yes, and today we - "

She cut me off with "Your father and I bought a house this weekend," she said.

"We setup the badminton set...wait, what?"

"In New Hampshire."

"New Hampshire?"

I only knew it from the two times we had gone up there for vacation.

"We leave in two days."

I was trying to follow her words.

My brain scrambled.

"We are moving," she said, "to New Hampshire."

Her tone sounded irritated now, like I wasn't getting it.

My feet went ice cold.

My eyes jumped from the photos of smiling people on the wall to the railing along the stairs to the black and white tile to my feet.

I couldn't feel my feet.

"But I have another month here with Hope and the kids."

Mom talked over me, as if I had said nothing,

"Hope has agreed to release you from your so-called baby-sitting job there a month early."

"What?"

My hands got cold.

In that moment, someone else was holding the phone.

It wasn't my hand anymore.

"*Moving?*" My brain screamed.

It was like that recurring nightmare I had in first grade where I would scream in the downstairs front hall bathroom, but no sound would come out.

"You will be going to the public school."

"Can't I stay where I am?"

I loved my school that I had attended forever. Although I was only in 8th grade, I had classes in Latin, French, Music, American Literature, History, Creative Writing, Gymnastics and Painting. And my best friends in the world: Joy, Susan and Maggie.

"What about my friends, and school, and

gymnastics?" I asked.

"It's all set."

Then as if talking about the weather, her tone went from irritable-serious to cheery-light, and she switched subjects as she would for the many painful years ahead.

"I understand your brother caught bluefish today!"

I squeezed my eyes tight until I saw spots behind my eyelids.

"Well no, actually, it was Larry, Hope's brother who caught fish today. I am going to cook them up in butter just like I did with the baby blues I caught last summer off the pier, remember?"

She sniffed and then, "Well, you enjoy that dear. You know, I never really liked bluefish, only swordfish for me. And that Larry...he drinks too much."

My face got hot. My eyes moved from the generations of Hope's family photos along the staircase to the stairs to the floor, the banister, trying to focus. Trying to force my brain to catch up.

I had the sensation I had stepped out of time.

My throat was closing-up on me, in a whisper I asked,

"Why can't I stay here? Why do I need to leave now?"

Maybe she did not hear me, maybe I did not even say it out loud, but what she said was, "OK dear, we will see you tomorrow. Bye, bye."

The hallway had grown darker in the last couple minutes. The sun had moved. I walked outside and stood on the front steps for a minute. Stiffening my body and taking a deep breath I tried my best to be a big girl, just get on with things like mom and dad had always taught me.

Benji ran up to me smiling he held out my badminton racquet to me.

Everything blurred.

My body heaved.

Then arms around me - catching me - Hope's arms. The same arms that showed me how to make snow angels.

Hope softly said to little Benji and Little Will looking on, "It's ok, she's just sad. How about you boys head over and see if you can go help Uncle Larry with those fish."

I was so embarrassed. I didn't want to cry. What a baby I was. I could hear my brother's heavy walk approaching in the grass, "What the hell happened?"

I was embarrassed to be crying in front of my brother.

I could feel the movement of Hope's arm waving him away.

Then to me, "Let's go sit over here for a minute."

She wrapped her arm around my shoulder and led me to the small side garden filled with roses. A red and pink blur through my tears. We sat on the cement garden bench. Gargoyles perched on either side of us.

"Ok," Hope said, "tell me what happened."

My brain had just stalled out. I didn't understand what was happening. It was all so sudden. "We're... moving...I guess?"

She stared back towards the house, scratching her left knee.

"I know," she said. "Your Mom asked me if you could leave early before the summer's out. She asked me if I could get a replacement to help with the kids."

"But I want to stay."

I had stopped crying now. I wanted her to look at me, and yet I didn't. I was embarrassed by my puffy eyes, my nose and face all red and gross.

Maybe this was just a bad dream, and I would wake up to find myself under thick quilts in my room at the end of the hallway.

Everyone said the fresh bluefish and salad that we ate at dinner were delicious.

I could not taste a thing.

※ ※ ※

After the boys were both tucked-in and read to, Hope and I went to my room to brush my hair as she'd promised.

Both sitting on my bed, I studied the room to memorize it, knowing that was the last night I would see it. I loved that room. Exposed wood walls. The nightstand a pale green with 19th century wood showing through on the worn spots. The knotty, woven rug on the floor – of blues, greens and purples like the sea glass colors Little Will and I cherished.

The dormer window was open. Crickets pulsed their evening song in a poetic rhythm.

I had fallen into the rhythm of the meaning of "family" that I had not known until that summer and I did not want to leave. It felt so safe. So full of laughter and joy and the newness of belonging.

Hope had been so kind to give me the job. She was paying me real money per week to look after my nephews and play games and have fun. It was a huge gift, and I would do whatever she asked me to, and joyfully.

If she wanted me to help her make sandwiches for the kids, she would show me how they liked them, and then I would be the sandwich maker whenever she asked.

Load the dishwasher, ok.

Read certain books to the boys while she ran errands, no problem.

I learned the foods they liked and would prepare lunch and sometimes all meals for the boys while she and my brother took time for themselves all afternoon and into the evening.

I learned so much from her and it was never through shame or criticism but rather by her example and encouragement, and sometimes gentle correction, with an occasional well-deserved ribbing, like when I tossed Benji's cobalt blue socks in with a load of white bedsheets. But she was never harsh or razor-critical like my mother often was.

At the same time Hope was building my self-confidence and showing me how to take on increasing responsibility, she also was a mother to me.

Like brushing or braiding my hair. I could not recall the last time my mother showed me that kind of nurturing affection and care.

"Did you like that new de-tangler?"

"Yes," I said, "it smells like strawberries."

"Yes, and it made your hair shiny and soft." She kept the bristles moving through my long hair. It felt so good. Simple warm comfort of a mother and daughter.

I picked at a stray thread on the quilt and I remembered how different it was with my Mom. There would be no more Hope brushing my hair that summer. No more warmth.

"Do you remember the first time you brushed my hair?" I asked.

Hope laughed. "Yes," she said, "it took awhile...you were quite a feral child with that tangle of hair."

Back then, years ago when I was just five, that was the first time. She had to cut out a snarl at the base of my skull behind my right ear the size of a quarter. She did it skillfully so you couldn't tell what was missing unless you lifted up my hair and looked for the gap. I never told anyone.

"Well, I was just a kid then," I said.

"Yes" she said.

Her hands were long and delicate yet strong. An imprint. A positive, nurturing one.

"You were much younger then."

She tugged the brush a little and leaned-in, "now that you are a young lady you can remember to brush your hair like this *every* night like this? One hundred strokes, OK?"

"OK," I said.

I started to tear up again. I hated being such a baby.

She placed her other hand on my back, directly behind my heart and said,

"You are a strong, beautiful and intelligent young woman. Promise me you will remember that. You can always call or write. We will come visit."

Her hand dropped away and she continued brushing my hair. I never saw Hope cry, ever, but her voice changed, as if she was choking up a bit too, "You know your brother and I... love you very much...always will."

"I know," I said.

But I didn't know.

In that moment all I knew was that the happiness I felt all those days at the Cape would now be behind me.

It reminded me of when Little Will and I would play during the holidays and mom would accuse us of being tired. *Nap time, you two!*

I was about to leave my best friends, my school my home, everything that I had always known and for the first time in my life I felt respected, seen, and valued for something other than my grades on my report card or how well-mannered I behaved when mom and dad showed me off at their cocktail and dinner parties.

This was a new lesson one of being given the serious real responsibility of taking care of others, and also I was deeply cared for, respected and nurtured by Hope.

That was all a very positive imprint, but that day, during just those few minutes on the phone with my mom, the older, competing imprint got bigger, deeper and became one that I would live out over and over again for years trying to fix.

The message seeped into my subconscious that I did not deserve to have that kind of happiness. I did not belong in such love.

That kind of safety and heart-bursting joy of that idyllic July was for someone else and if by mistake I had it, the moment was fleeting or worse I would be punished for being so ebulliently happy.

I had found family, found a sense of belonging and love. Now, it would be taken away.

So too it seemed almost worse to know the feeling and then have it taken away than to never know it at all.

My eyes stung from crying so much. I couldn't hear the crickets anymore, just the sound of blood rushing in my ears. She pulled me into to the softness of her bright yellow sundress.

Her tan arms enveloped me and she rocked me gently like a baby.

I didn't want to leave this. Leave them.

Leave our afternoon naps when we all snoozed in the sunlight or laughed in ticklefest dog piles.

The loud, family game nights of Clue, Life or Yahtzee when Benji would dance around the room with my brother's baseball cap, chanting "Yahtzee, Yaht-zee! Yaaah-tz-zeeee!" in between turns no matter which game we were playing.

Or when my brother showed me how to buddy breathe for the first time in deep water using his scuba tank.

Or when Benji would embellish the story of Robin Hood insisting that Maid Marian and Princess Leia of Star Wars were actually sisters. And that only *his* closet was the real one that went to Narnia.

Or how Little Will liked it best when I made his egg salad sandwiches with a layer of sliced pickels.

"I don't want to move," I said.

I turned and looked back at Hope. She put the brush down, and hugged me again letting me cry until I stopped.

It felt so safe, so right, so foreign.

She put a new box of tissues by the bed and tucked me in. Kissed me goodnight on my forehead like she did when I was younger and turned out the light.

❋ ❋ ❋

The next morning, I woke to the soft sunlight and faint sound of a mourning dove's coo outside my window.

Safe and peaceful.

And then, the slow waking recall seeped into my consciousness of the day before. I pulled Hope's grandmother's patchwork quilt up over my head.

Downstairs, my brother, Hope, and the kids were eating breakfast.

"I made waffles," Hope said.

I sat down at the table in silence. I put on a smile. I did not want to cry again.

My brother was asking the questions I had wanted to ask but didn't.

I finally jumped in and spoke,

"What about my bedroom? I have to pack the stuff in my bedroom don't I?"

"No," Hope repeated what she said to my brother, "your mom said that the movers already packed the *whole* house. All of it. They are loading the truck today."

The thought of a strange man rifling through my underwear drawer went through my head,

"My clothes. My books?"

"Yes," she said, "All packed."

My brother, William, looked at me.

"Damn," he said as he pushed his chair away from the table and walked back into kitchen.

"Any more waffles?"

"In the oven," Hope said.

My brother came back out, kissed Little Will and Benji on their heads, and sat down a plate heaped high with warm golden brown perfect waffles.

I could barely look up at these faces of a happy family. A lump of tears in my throat, but I did not want to cry again. Not in front of the boys. I had to be strong. I wanted to remember this summer always.

Benji insisted he could cut his waffles without his parent's help using a smaller size butter knife.

Little Will ate in silence for several bites, taking it all in, and then looked across the table at me and said,

"Well…if there are lakes near grandpa and grandma's we could still go snorkeling and fishing next summer."

"That's a great idea, buddy," I smiled "I am going to miss you guys so much."

I looked over at Hope hoping to hear her

say, "Your mom and I talked again last night, and you are staying here until September as planned."

But she didn't say that.

Instead, she held out the serving plate and said, "Waffle?"

DEATH AT 14

That dark Wednesday evening in late October, I heard my sister Lydia's voice unlike I had ever heard it before.
"Lydia, what's wrong?" I asked
"Please. Just put Mom on the phone."
Mom sensed something was not right because instead of her normal cheery greeting of, "Hello Dear, how are things?" she took the phone and said, "Lydia - what's wrong?"
I could hear my sister crying and her muffled words, "He's dead."
Mom steadied herself with her hand on the kitchen counter.
"OK," Mom said, "I'm putting your father

on the phone."

She handed him the receiver. His blue eyes looked little boy scared, but his voice and body were all business.

He listened, then, "We will be on the first flight tomorrow."

When he hung up the phone, he took one breath, and reached for the thin yellow pages in the kitchen drawer.

Mid-dial, he hung up, turned to me and said,

"We'll have to have you stay with someone."

"Who will she stay with," mom asked, "we don't know anyone here yet."

There we were. The three of us.

New state, new home, new lives.

No friends.

Mom and dad had been quite social as soon as we'd arrived holding an open house before Labor Day and attending cocktail and dinner parties quite often. Leaving me alone most evenings while they connected with dad's network from his college and graduate school days.

And I, still so new at my school, I had not developed any real friendships yet either.

So there we were, me and my middle-aged stoic parents in stunned silence.

And then it was one of those moments where my whole body knew it before my brain registered how to say it. I blurted out in a tone of uncharacteristic defiance,

"She's my sister. And I'm going."

I walked upstairs to my bedroom, without waiting for their response or approval and started packing.

Hours before dawn, we were all in the car on our the way to the airport.

※ ※ ※

When mom opened the bedroom door in their apartment the first thing I noticed was the smell.

The dog smelled it. He walked by the open bedroom door, black wet nose towards the room, then pulled his tail in tight to his rump, and scurried away.

The bed was just as the coroner had left it - blankets were bunched up on the right side of the bed where my sister usually slept. The top sheet was pulled back.

Stains.

There were stains on the white sheets. Remnants of Eric, brick red, brown and faint yellow. The brown was smeared as if the body was a brush on canvas.

I felt sick to my stomach. I swallowed and pointed to the sheets, "What's that," I asked.

Mom snapped on tight yellow kitchen gloves.

Snap. Snap.

She reached for his pillow and shook it from its case. Rust brown spots on the pillowcase. She threw the pillow on the floor, tossed the case on top of it.

"That pillow will have to be thrown out," Mom said.

She hated waste. She had been a depression era child who had to survive on two bowls of oatmeal a day, and wasted nothing, but even this could not be saved.

I walked towards the pillow to throw it out.

"Don't touch that," she said, "I'll do that."

She waved me back to the foot of the bed.

"Mom?" My voice quiet, as if I would wake someone.

"Yes?"

"What are those stains?"

Mom shook the other pillow out. Lydia's pillow. No stains. She wouldn't look at me.

"The body lets go after you die," she said, "grab that corner."

We pulled off the fitted sheet. Elastic corners snapped to the center.

"How could he die so young," I asked.

The stains had bled through to the mattress cover.

Mom pointed to the lower right corner of the bed.

"Pull that corner up over there."

I reached under the mattress, and peeled back the thick, tight elastic mattress cover.

"And how did she not know? The smell. I mean, she must have smelled it...right?"

With her yellow gloves, Mom folded the top sheet and bottom sheet in on themselves until the stain was hidden.

Then she pulled the four corners of the mattress cover up and around making a neat little bundle.

Stained cloth sagging with molecules of my 29 year old brother-in-law.

When she lifted the bundle of bedding off the bed, there was more. I swallowed down the sick feeling coming up from my stomach.

She paused and eyed the blue-striped mattress.

"We'll have to flip it," she said, and walked around the foot of the bed to the side where my sister usually slept.

Mom at the head, me at the foot, we lifted up the full-sized mattress on its side, then we pulled the opposite side out from under and it slapped down on the box spring.

"How could she not know he was dead before she kissed him?"

It was awful, and I could not understand it. My sister had been attending a two-day seminar for her new job and he had died in his sleep the one night she was away.

When she arrived home late that next evening to find the shades were drawn, the room was dark and she just leaned over to kiss him thinking he was asleep, but his lips were cold.

Mom walked over to the bundle of bedding and scooped it up in her arms. She walked out to the kitchen. I followed her.

She nodded towards the kitchen sink, "Get a garbage bag out. Please."

I opened the door under the sink, and pulled black plastic from the yellow box.

I shook open the plastic, and tried one more time, "And what about the dog - he was running around like crazy but refused to go in their bedroom. Mom, don't you think she knew something was wrong? Before, before she kissed him?"

I held open the garbage bag and she tipped her arms so that the fabric fell into the bag. Then she pushed the bedding down. Yellow gloves stuffing it in the black plastic bag.

She turned her head away. She snapped the rubber gloves off. Smell of sweat on powdery rubber on top of everything else, "Can't get blood stains out," she said, "now go wash your hands."

"Why is there blood?"

I stood there wanting mom to give me an answer. Anything to explain how such a thing could happen. How a young healthy man who ran several times a week would just die in his sleep.

Mom pulled the red plastic tape synching the bag up tight. Her fingers strained against the plastic ribbon tie wrapping the ribbon of red plastic around and around and around five or so times leaving just enough to tie a knot.

To make it air-tight.

To make sure nothing can come out.

She stood up straight.

Molecules of Eric wrapped in black plastic between our feet.

Finally, she looked at me directly, her brown eyes flat.

Her lips tight, "We will know more after the autopsy. There's no point in speculating," she said, "now go wash your hands."

She held the bag away from her body and walked towards the front door. The dog followed her out onto the porch. Small Mom, wool-slacked Mom, walked outside with a bag that looked more than half her size.

Washing my hands in the kitchen sink I heard the metal trash can cover scrape open and the sound of plastic slipping against metal.

The bedding was gone, but the smell stuck in my nose. I went into the bedroom, pulled the blind cord, and opened the two small windows to let in some air. *How could she not smell it? How could she not know something was wrong?*

Dad left after he had been on the phone with Eric's family from Vancouver. They discussed funeral arrangements, and decided to have an autopsy since it was not normal for a healthy man of 29 to die in his sleep.

* * *

By late afternoon mom was still cleaning. The sliding shower door slammed back and forth, back and forth.

Crisp, leather shoes on tile, then on hardwood floor. Mom stood across the linoleum table from Lydia, holding a clear-handled toothbrush.

I knew that toothbrush, and I knew not to touch it. Just like the Michigan State sweatshirt hanging on the hook by the front door...not to be touched.

"I'm going to throw this out," mom said.

Lydia pushed her long black hair back from her face, stood up, and ripped the toothbrush out of mom's hand. She walked into the bathroom.

Mom followed her, and stood in the bathroom doorway, arms crossed in front of her.

If this were Mrs. Brady and Marcia, Mrs. Brady would hold her daughter and try to comfort her.

But my mom was not Mrs. Brady. My mom was bred from the harsh, winter light of strong, New England stock. She felt things very deeply, but had been taught to not show emotions to anyone except my father.

I walked over to the kitchen table.

The three of us now beads angled on a necklace.

My sister at the sink.

Mom, standing in the bathroom doorway.

And me, in the long shadow of Mom.

Lydia picked up the mug from the narrow glass shelf, placed Eric's toothbrush back inside next to hers, and sat the mug down without a sound.

Mom stretched her right leg back behind her. The dog started to pace behind her.

To be anyplace but here. Anyplace but in the middle of this thick, heavy sadness.

"Your father is meeting with the minister about the funeral. Do you want to go to the church and meet the minister?"

Church.

Mom believed that faith, prayer and a strong work ethic could get you through anything.

At 14 I had a vague idea of faith at best, and

a distaste for 'religion'.

* * *

I was kicked out of Sunday school at the ripe old age of six for asking too many questions.

When the topic of "Father, Son, and Holy Spirit" came up I had asked,

"Why is Jesus with only his father in heaven?"

A low murmur and controlled giggles came from the boys sitting in the row next to me.

"Because that is what scripture tells us," she said.

"But where is the mother?"

"You just have to believe," she said, "and have faith in the Father, Son and Holy Spirit."

At my regular school, we were taught to ask questions if we don't understand, so I raised my hand again earnestly wanting the truth.

"But wouldn't Jesus' mom also be in heaven when she died?"

After a few more of my questions about Mary, it was clear I was confused, but the teacher could not answer me other than saying you have to have faith. But I had a mother and father, and if Jesus had a mother and father, why was he only in heaven with Father, and the Holy Spirit.

Then I asked the question that really got me in trouble,

"Is the Holy Spirit the ghost of Mary?"

In my mind it made sense, that way Jesus would be in heaven with both his parents, and that was all I was trying to understand.

Where was his mother?

The teacher's solution was to lock me in the coat closet for the remainder of the class. I whimpered in the dark, and tried to not gag on the sharp stench of mothballs.

When mom came to get me after church, they had let me out. I was a red-faced, scared and tear-stained mess.

I pointed to the coat closet and told her, "They put me in there."

"What did you do to make them do that?" Mom asked me.

The teacher approached my mother with perfect politeness and explained,

"I'm sorry but your daughter was being disruptive and I gave her a time-out. No harm done."

"I am so sorry," my mother apologized, "she has always been my most inquisitive child."

"How are Lydia and George? They were always such attentive and intelligent students"

The teacher looked down at me with a flash of contempt, "Very well-behaved."

"Thank you," mom responded while fixing my coat, "Lydia is spending a year on exchange in France and George was accepted at Yale, Dartmouth *and* Harvard!"

"I would expect nothing less," she said, "please give them my best, I thoroughly enjoyed having them in class."

Mom fussed with my scarf and tied it a bit too snug.

"Perhaps this one is a late bloomer, maybe wait another year or two?"

They shook hands and then mom followed up with, "I am so sorry for your trouble, it won't happen again."

Mom squeezed my hand and pulled us towards the door. The same boys who had sat in the row next to me were standing around the doorway. They made faces at me and said,

"Cry baby... Such a guurrlll."

My mother in her crimson embarrassment did not hear it, or pretended not to.

"Do not tell your father what happened," she said as we walked fast down the corridor, "I will talk to him. And he will decide what to do."

My parents still insisted I go to church but instead of Sunday School classes, I sat with them in the pew for almost two hours. I noticed the people around me, frowning faces, fancy hats, lines of the oak grain, the frayed edges of the books, the texture of velvet. The organ music sounded so awful and depressing, but singing I liked.

When the grey old man would yell at us from a wooden box high up on the wall, I would look up, but did not understand anything he said. My neck hurt after service.

Mom and dad liked to go for cookies and coffee in the meeting hall after service, and now I went with them. It wasn't much better.

Almost every Sunday, the creepy minster in his long robes would make a point of coming over to speak with my parents.

He would pat my head and stroke my long hair and say, "What a pretty young lady you are." Or he would make a point of what I was wearing, "What a lovely dress you have on today. Very fine."

He was fat and smelled funny.

I began to dislike my long hair and my dresses.

I figured out how to time my request for a cookie until I saw him headed towards us. Once at the refreshment table, I would go slow and wait long enough for him to finish talking with my folks. He seemed to have caught on to this because he began to come over twice, and I was never allowed a second cookie, so then I would ask my father if I could get him a cookie. If dad said no, I made an effort to stand in-between my mother and father so that I would be harder for the minister's hands to reach.

He still tried.

That was the year I learned that my school was different than other classrooms, and asking too many questions or the wrong ones will get little girls locked in closets.

Or worse.

By fourteen I still believed in God in a general sense, and the joys of Christmas in particular.

As for my exposure to death, my grandmother passed away when I was eleven. I was not allowed to attend her open-casket funeral, but mom asked me to help her clean out her house. It took us most of the summer.

Day after day we sorted the evidence of Grammy's life into either boxes for storage, or trash or public auction.

To mom's shock, I found several empty gin bottles in random places. They were tucked under her mattress, in the shoeboxes of her wardrobe, in the attic under the window, and in the drawers of my father's desk he used as a boy.

She had a house full of beautiful things: always fresh flowers in porcelain vases, small and large hand-painted clocks that chimed on the quarter hour in different tones, thick colorful oriental rugs under a beautiful Steinway grand piano, where she played Chopin for me. Delicate porcelain figurines kept her books company on the shelves, and the doors to her sunroom were held open by cast iron doorstops that were painted to look like sitting French Bulldogs.

Grammy's photos, travel journals and the deeply poetic love letters she received betrayed her stylish and poised demeanor.

My grandmother did not even have the right to vote, but she learned to play piano beautifully, studied Italian, French, Greek and Latin; read Jane Austen, George Elliot, Keats, Byron and Wordsworth. She took photos of Byron's Bridge of Sighs in Venice with her very own Brownie snapshot camera, and sketched Bernini's Elephant in the Piazza della Minerva when she was in Rome.

She found the Roman Forum "too unbearably hot" to spend the day looking at "mostly dull piles of stone and random broken columns", but she fell in love with Botticelli's *Birth of Venus* in Florence and wrote that she found "painters to be much more interesting than poets."

Photos of her with her classmates on the streets of Rome and Paris - young women dressed in heavy Victorian clothing with large fancy hats and hands covered in gloves.

After her rare and privileged education, she returned to America to marry and settle into her role as wife and mother only to be widowed very young. Dad was only a teenager, and yet suddenly when his father died, he became the 'man of the house'. In later years she found comfort in her son's weekly visits, her grandchildren, and her increasing attachment to Gin Martinis.

Cocktails were introduced to society during her lifetime, and as a young bride she learned how to serve them at their elaborate parties, but after her husband died, grief was her constant companion, and it didn't matter whether she had company for cocktails or not.

At some point her comfort became addiction and what seemed fun and glamorous when she was young ultimately led to her painful death.

To me she was the much older grandmother who gave me wonderful Steiff stuffed animals at Christmas; served me root beer floats with vanilla ice cream in the summertime; and played Chopin for me on her piano while I daydreamed surrounded by beautiful things. It was the good the true and the beautiful to be in her home that was bright and airy full of light and color.

Hers was positive imprint that informed my love of creativity, classical art and beauty.

I would ride my bike to her house and sometimes she would come to our house to babysit me, but increasingly she would wear her sunglasses inside even at the dinner table.

During the last year of her life, she babysat me the night of a big thunderstorm that would be the last time mom and dad asked her to look after me. She sat in my desk chair in the middle of my bedroom. Frozen. The thunder became louder as the storm approached and the flashes of lightning lit up my bedroom windows with increasing frequency.

"Grammy what's wrong?"

"Stay away from the windows," she said.

She would not move. She just sat there in the center of my room in her navy wool dress, red silk scarf and dark sunglasses until the storm ended.

She didn't babysit me after that, and I was afraid of thunderstorms for years to come, but I would still ride my bike over to visit her, and then, a few months later, she died.

A sad and tragic end that I did not understand at eleven, but I did grasp that death came to her when she was very old.

Grandparents grew old and older people were supposed to die, that was the nature of things, but not healthy young men who jogged several times a week and loved my sister.

Why did God allow such a vital young man in the prime of his life to die and cause such pain for those left behind?

And in his sleep.

That made it all even scarier because I had never heard of a young person dying in their sleep.

* * *

My sister closed her eyes. Her hands on porcelain, she leaned into the pedestal sink. I wanted her to rip the sink from the wall.

For someone to *do* something.

Anything, to show some emotion…some life.

I leaned into the robins-egg blue linoleum kitchen table and pressed my fingers hard into the aluminum edge.

I wanted metal to enter flesh.

Half-breaths make you invisible.

The apartment was cold. No insulation. My sister looked so small in her husband's robe. She was not the same woman who got married on my thirteenth birthday.

We will always remember the date. Now my birthday would be a reminder to her of not just their wedding day, but also his death, and this pain.

The five feet of white tile floor separating Mom and Lydia looked big, clean and shiny.

Lydia was wearing his brown wool socks. *Blood on sheets.*

Lydia took a breath bigger than herself, keeping her head down she pushed by Mom in the bathroom doorway.

"Leave the toothbrush alone. Just leave it Mother."

She sat down at the kitchen table behind me, pawing mindlessly through random envelopes. The bills she'd been paying cluttered the table.

"What is it you and Dad always say? Work will get you through?"

Mom walked over to the kitchen sink and picked up a sponge and turned on the water.

It seemed it was only a matter of minutes before Mom would suggest that the dog go for another walk. She would say something like,

"The dog looks like he needs to go out. It's

so cruel to keep him locked up in here."

Or something like that, but never that mom needed air, or that it was cruel to keep us locked up in here.

In there.

Inside ourselves.

Alone. Together.

The wall heater made snapping sounds of metal expanding. My stomach nausea and cold hands. So many more feelings to ignore. Eight of my fingertips had deep indentations from the edge of the table. Imprints.

All of this an imprint.

* * *

Midnight.

Lydia and I huddled under the thick, old quilts of the narrow guest bed. Her tears a slow wet through my nightgown. Her jaw moved against my shoulder and collarbone as she spoke,

"I was rushing to catch my plane to the conference that morning, and he wanted to make love."

My neck still bare in the dark chill of the room. She sucked her tears back in.

Her voice so quiet I could barely hear.

"I pushed him away. Told him there was no time."

She reached her hand across my waist. Her hand fidgeted with the sleeve of my flannel nightgown.

"He looked at me with those green-grey eyes, his hair all messy."

The sound of spit stuck on her tongue mixed with her words.

"Then he leaned over me, and whispered, 'C'mon, just a quickie.'"

Ever since her exchange year in France when she was seventeen, and I was only six, Lydia was very comfortable and open about the topic of sex. So comfortable to the point of having a heavy make-out session with her boyfriend on my bed that following summer when she was supposed to be babysitting me. She stopped when I walked-in on them only to laugh at my embarrassment and say, "Oh don't be such a prude!"

So comfortable as to explain in detail about how in France they "French kiss", and then there was the awkward time at Christmas one year when she questioned me about masturbation when I was too young to even know what the word meant.

But this, this was even more uncomfortable.

And then I felt guilty for feeling uncomfortable.

One tear lined my face cold down to the pillowcase. My throat hurt. I wanted to roll over and cry, but knew I had to be strong for her. She needed me to be the strong little sister, not the baby.

Her voice went away again, "I should have stayed," she said quietly, "How was I to know it was the last chance we'd ever have to be together?"

Pressing cloth.

She twisted the flannel of my sleeve tighter and tighter pinching my skin with it. Her body shook against mine with tears. I stroked her hair, trying to comfort her. Sadness mixed with guilt, salty tears and snot.

✶ ✶ ✶

The last time I saw Eric alive was their first and last Christmas as husband and wife.

Mom and dad and I had spent it with them, in this very apartment.

Christmas Eve, we went to a professor's party near campus. Tall Eric wore his forest green corduroy jacket with gray wool slacks. And those boots. Boots were the only shoes he owned besides his running sneakers.

A brilliant grad student with a promising future, he stood tall at the fireplace with his brandy on the mantle next to his right elbow, his left hand holding a spear in the fire. Roasting chestnuts and talking with two other students. Three spears roasting chestnuts in the fireplace.

Lydia and I sat on the couch a few feet away. He gave her that look.

That look that made me re-cross my legs.

He mouthed something to her about "getting her" later.

She laughed, turned to me and put her hand on my knee,

"Hey, is it OK if we break our tradition and don't sleep in the same bed this year?"

Her brown eyes - soft chestnut brown. In love eyes. In love eyes that went away forever after he died.

Lydia and I had this tradition to sleep in the same bed Christmas Eve, and Santa would deliver our stockings to the foot of the bed in the middle of the night.

We would spend the early pre-dawn hours opening our stockings together. Each item individually wrapped in green or red tissue paper and tied with thin ribbon. Even if it was obvious in its wrapping - like a toothbrush or the triangular shaped Toblerone chocolate, we'd giggle and ask each other "what could this be?"

After reaching the small canvas bag that held US Mint copper pennies in the toe of the stocking, we would carefully put each of the presents back into our stockings, and try to fall back to sleep until an acceptable hour.

But we never slept. We would catch up on school, her real boyfriends and my dreams of having one someday.

We talked and laughed, our faces inches apart on the pillows of my bed. Our stockings with crumpled red and green tissue and ribbons strewn around at the end of the bed like a Cubist painting.

That last Christmas, I became the jealous little sister,

"But we *always* do our stockings together, and we did it last year."

"Well Eric and I were not married yet last

Christmas were we?" She said to me while smiling at him.

She rocked my knee back and forth, "We could open them together in the morning. It will be just like always."

"It's not the same," I said.

I hated myself for being such a brat. He was watching us. His forefinger tapped the chestnut at the end of the fire poker to see if it was done.

She looked over at him, "Eric?"

She moved her hand off my knee, and folded her hands in her lap.

Eric walked toward us with that big grin of his and floppy perfect hair.

"Yesssss," he said.

Lydia nervously smoothed her green Pendleton skirt over her knees.

"Getting our stockings together is kind of a tradition with us. Is it OK if you and I sleep apart just for tonight?"

His eyes over to me, then to back to her, "That's cool."

He smiled that big wide-jaw smile of his. His firm cheeks accordioned up behind the corners of his mouth.

Then he did that look, right *at* her. It was

just a look, but so intimate it made my face hot.

"I'm sure we'll have plenty of Christmases together," he said.

✳ ✳ ✳

Now, in this same drafty apartment, in the same guest bedroom where she and I had slept that Christmas eve, it had become the place where they would have no more Christmases.

Lydia's voice in low tones.

Then slow and clear she said, "Remember this: everything and everyone you ever love will be taken from you."

...

End of Book 1

EMOTIONAL IMPRINTS SERIES

The Emotional Imprints series explores one person's search for love, identity, and meaning. What shapes a life, what makes a person who they are? Are one's emotional imprints ever truly knowable? If they can be identified and understood, can a person change the course of their life, or will they be forever subconsciously chained to those imprints of the past?

Dinosaurs & Snow Angels

The first book of the series, Dinosaurs & Snow Angels, Early Stories, focuses on Beth Lawrence's childhood and early adolescence, and the emotional imprints that influence her development and shape the future struggles she will have to overcome to discover her true authentic self.

Pitch, Yaw & Roll

In Pitch, Yaw & Roll, book two of the Emotional Imprints Series, we find Beth Lawrence tossed into the unknown. "New state, new home, new lives. No friends." What secrets are her parents keeping from her, and why did Eric die so young?

ACKNOWLEDGEMENTS

Although a writer spends hour upon hour and day after day alone, a writer is never truely alone. Haunted by ghosts, loved by angels, and cajoled by characters who appear on the page as if by magic, the writer finds home. Je suis, I am. This book would not be possible without the lessons and challenges of life's mentors and teachers, and the encouragement of many including my beloved mother and father. And to one in particular: I say, "Thank you 'my Hemingway', we did it."

Made in the USA
Las Vegas, NV
30 June 2021